Death at the

Summit

Nikki Haverstock

DEDICATION

To John Haverstock, who didn't let me throw my
computer off a mountain when I got frustrated.

CONTENTS

ACKNOWLEDGMENTS

Special thanks to Zara Keane and Zoe York who helped me put all the information into action. I owe you both hugs and endless drinks.

To my supportive family, thank you for only being slightly shocked when I said I was going to write a book.

Thank you to the Archery community—without you, I wouldn't have a setting or any villains. Especially, Teresa Johnson who is my archery partner-in-crime and double-checks that my fictional archery world doesn't get too out there.

Thank you to Lori, Holly, and AJ, who give me a private place to vent so I don't make a fool of myself in public.

Thank you to my amazing cover artist and editing team: you are the ones that made the book shine.

Nikki Haverstock

When opportunity "nocks"…

When a new Westwood employee with old grudges is murdered during the brand summit, Di starts investigating with roommate Mary and Great Dane Moo at her side. After a snowstorm strands all the suspects at the Westmound Center and the only cop present asks Di and Mary not to get in the way, they have to keep a low profile.

It's no surprise that Mac was murdered. He was a sexist bigot who used his business to take advantage of others prior to being bought out by Westmound. With so many suspects, will they be able to find the real killer?

A wholesome cozy murder for every sleuth in the family

"Funny, charming, and occasionally deadly." ~ NYT bestselling author Zoe York

Target Practice Mysteries #2

CHAPTER ONE

I entered the conference room of the Westmound Center for Competitive Shooting Sports a few minutes before the scheduled meeting. The meeting was supposed to be for all the people working range day for the Westmound Summit, which started the next day, but I was the only person there, along with Moo, my loaner dog while I am at the center.

The room had several rows of tables with chairs that faced a wall covered in whiteboards. Along the top of the boards were paper chains made from construction paper. Our evening television watching in the unit I shared with my roommate, Mary, had been transformed into craft time. The paper chains we'd made weren't the traditional ones of people holding hands, but long lines of bows, both recurve and compounds, and a variety of guns.

Every week when went we went to church with Liam, Mary insisted that we pick up just a few more things, and the entire center had been transformed into an explosion of Christmas and holiday decorations. Mary was obsessed with decorating.

There was a real tree in the corner that barely reached my shoulder and was straining under the weight of our handmade ornaments. It was enswathed in lace-covered, bead-studded little plastic guns and red and green army men, each with a little felt Santa hat. Moo trotted over to the tree and sniffed the glittered popcorn strands that hung on it. His fuzzy lips twitched, and he extended them toward the chain.

"Moo, get over here," I called to him. He slowly came over to me, casting longing looks over his shoulder at the tree, as I pulled out a chair at the front table and faced the whiteboard.

The windows in the room were covered in sticky

window clings proclaiming Merry Christmas. Outside, snowflakes fell slowly, completing the image of the perfect Christmas season that I had been raised to imagine by television and movies. This would be my first winter with snow, and I had already spent hours staring out the window.

I scratched behind Moo's large ears, which were propping up a tiny Santa's hat. He perfectly matched the harlequin Great Dane gracing my shirt, though Moo was not decorated with lights and ornaments the way the dog on my shirt was.

Jess raced into the room, her pursed lips at odds with her whimsical Christmas shirt with reindeer drinking from wine glasses. It was silly-sweater week at the Westmound Center for Competitive Shooting Sports as part of our celebration before the center closed for Christmas break.

She stomped over to the whiteboard while looking at her notebook, then started writing out a list on the board. "Thank you all for coming. I'm in a rush, so please pay attention while I pass out your assignments."

"Hey, I hate to break it to—"

Jess cut me off with a raised hand over her shoulder as she continued to write. "Not now, Di. We have a lot of things to get through, and we can't waste everyone's time with your jokes."

I snorted. It was true that often I couldn't keep myself from being a snarky goof-off, but right now was not one of those moments. In the handful of weeks I had worked at the center, the staff had become a casual family, especially those who worked on the archery side of the center. Jess and I had been friends since college. We both chose to attend an excellent Texas university with an active archery program. The members of the team were roomed together. Knowing each other for so long allowed some leniency in how we talked to each other.

"Turn around, Curly."

Jess whipped around, her dark curling hair bouncing, with a huge gasp, then looked around the empty room. "Where is everyone?"

The last event at the center, a coaches' course, had ended in murder, and Jess had been working overtime to make sure the event was perfect. Tomorrow, the Westmound Summit started. At the yearly event, employees from Westmound and Westmound subsidiaries came together to show off their new products and talk about the Westmound brand.

Normally, it was held in Salt Lake, but this year, we were hosting it in Wyoming because Westmound wanted to show off its new state-of-the-art training facility.

I shrugged at her.

"I'm exhausted," said Jess. "This time, everything needs to go perfectly." She checked her phone then pulled a chair around the table to sit opposite me. She sagged into her chair before grabbing a piece of paper out of her notebook. "I have something for you. This is the list of archery equipment you should get."

She slid the piece of paper across the table to me. I had started shooting archery again with beginner equipment I was borrowing from the range. My roommate, Mary, had been joining me on the range for daily practice. We had both taken a break from shooting—her for a year and me for eight years—but now we were hitting the range daily. Jess was the elite training coach at the center and had been working with both of us. My old equipment was long gone, except for my finger tab, and Jess had offered to recommend equipment once I was back at the level where I needed it.

The list included riser length, limb length and draw weight, stabilizer lengths, as well as everything I would need for a full competition setup, but nowhere did it list what brand or model. My confusion must have shown because Jess turned the list so she could see it, too.

"This is a good starter set up that we can adjust as you figure out what you like. I modeled it on what the Koreans are shooting. That's what we talked about, right?"

I nodded. The Korea Women's recurve team was a dominant force in competitive archery and if it was good enough for them, then it was good enough for me. "But there aren't any brands or model names on the list."

She slumped back in her chair, scrubbing her hand through her hair a few times before rubbing her eyes. "I have a suggestion for that, but don't feel any pressure. I was going to recommend that you stick to Westmound products. They're the best in the world, and you do work for them, so…"

"Yes, totally. I'd love to do that." In the short time I had worked for them, they had taken great care of me. After finding a body last month, the center owner, Elizabeth, had personally arranged for me to meet with a local counselor and called once or twice to ask if I liked my job, if I needed anything, or had suggestions to improve technology at the center since that was my job.

"Westmound products are amazing. I want you to ask Liam what he recommends." Liam's job description was the rather vague-sounding title of equipment guy. Many people in the industry called him Lumberjack, but after he confided that he preferred his real name, my friends and I had switched to Liam.

Jess checked her watch one more time then pulled out her phone. "I'm going to call everyone and see why they aren't here."

I grabbed Moo, who was wiggling around on the ground to scratch his back, and slipped through the door with the list. Maybe Liam was in the equipment room, and I could get him a copy of the list. I had barely seen him since Mary, Liam, and I had attended church last Sunday. Usually, we would share a meal with some friends at the center cafeteria a few days a week or have a variety of conversations in the hallway, but he had been busy preparing for the summit late into the night then sleeping in. I knew because I not-so-casually asked whenever I encountered one of the firearms guys he hung out with.

Moo darted ahead then ran back and leaned up against me as I walked. After repeating this three times,

I stopped and grabbed his face. His head was just above my waist, and I only had to lean over a little to look him in the eyes. "You're going to knock me over one of these days." I couldn't help but pepper the top of his head with kisses.

I released him, and he bounded and bounced all over the hallway with his tongue hanging out and the corners of his mouth pulled up into a grin.

On my first day of work, Moo had moved into my office to get away from the sound of gunfire on the other side of the horseshoe-shaped center that I worked in. We had become fast friends, and I thought of him as my dog even though he belonged to Liam, who fed him and gave him a place to sleep at night.

I rounded the corner and approached the room marked Equipment.

Moo hopped into the room, but I hung back at the door to observe Liam for the time it took him to turn. He was the epitome of the strong, silent type. Mary said he had a reputation for not talking, but I didn't find that to be true, as we often chatted. He was taller than I was, with a full beard that he confessed he only trimmed in winter when he started zipping it into his jacket. His hair was short on the sides and longer on top, somewhere

8

between a Mohawk and a military flattop. He had light eyes somewhere between green and blue. Maybe one day I would be able to get close enough to discern which.

I watched his hands deftly assemble a gun on the counter until Moo shoved his head between Liam and the counter. Liam looked around, and when we locked eyes, he gave me a quick smile and waved me into the room.

He turned back to finish his task. "Hey, on the corner of the table is a book for you."

A large worktable dominated the center of the room, and on the corner was a book that Mary and I had discussed last Sunday. I had mentioned wanting to read it. The cover of the paperback clung tight to the inner pages, and the spine was smooth. It appeared to be a brand-new copy. If he'd bought a copy just to loan it to me, then that was one of the sweetest things ever, but I shouldn't assume. Maybe he never read his copy or wanted a copy for himself. "Thank you. I'll return it when I am done."

Liam shrugged without turning around. The back of his neck was a little red. "No worries. I wish I could chat more, but I have a ton of work to do before tomorrow." He took the gun he had finished, put it into a case, then added it to a growing stack of cases on the far side of the table.

I folded the list, feeling a bit silly for interrupting him. I could wait until I returned from Christmas break. Moo returned to my side. "I totally understand. I'll catch you later." I turned to leave, a little embarrassed, my hand with the list at my side. Moo snatched the list from my hand and bounded across the room, banging into the back of Liam's knee.

He reached down to Moo's mouth and gave him a firm command. "Drop it." He looked over the list, and his eyes lit up. "Were you going to ask about equipment? I can squeeze in three minutes for that."

Three minutes of talking was better than nothing. "Jess says I am ready to order equipment and I should talk to you. I want to go with all Westmound equipment."

He looked back at me. "Are you sure you want to do that? You don't have to just because you work here."

"I want to."

He pocketed the list and gave me a smile. Then he leaned back on the table. "How is shooting going?"

"Awesome! I'm so glad to be shooting again. Mary

has started shooting again, too. Mostly, I have been focusing on basic form and building strength. I'm so excited to get my own setup and really start training."

Liam nodded along, then watched me for a few seconds before replying, "How serious are you?"

I was passionate about archery, and I wanted to train hard and shoot well, but I hesitated. My instinct was to say something offhand like "We'll see," or "It depends," but I knew that wasn't true. I hadn't expressed to anyone how badly I wanted to test myself and see what I was capable of. Maybe it was a need to prove myself after the divorce, some deep-seated urge to prove that I wasn't too old or perhaps to cash in on all the potential I'd had while on the college archery team. I started to step closer to him but caught myself and stood still.

"Very serious. I know I'm just beginning again and have a long way to go, but I really want…" I wasn't sure what I wanted, but I searched for the words to describe the ache in me.

Liam nodded, pushed off the counter, and walked toward me. "To know how good you can be?"

I nodded and smiled in the warmth of him knowing what I was trying to say. My smile broke wide across my face as he approached.

"Are you willing to train hard? Go to competitions? Work on your equipment?"

I laughed. "That sounds like heaven."

Liam laughed with me and checked his phone. "I've got to get going. I'll take care of the equipment, but it won't be until after the Westmound Summit is done." He went back to moving boxes and cases around the room.

I edged toward the door, not wanting to overstay my welcome. "Is there anything else that I need to order? Can I buy everything I need from Westmound?" I patted my leg, and Moo trotted over. I started rubbing behind his ears.

"Westmound doesn't make all these products directly, but it owns companies that do. The riser and limbs I recommend will come from Andersson Archery. They make the best competitive bows in the industry."

"Thanks for your help. I'll get out of your hair now." I turned to leave with Moo at my side.

He lifted a hand to stop. "Hold up. I've a favor to ask you, too. I have a ton of meetings. Can Moo stay with you tonight? Maybe longer?"

"Of course," I said.

"Moo, come here. I'll move this stuff then bring him back to you with his food and bowl. Where will you be for the next few hours?" Moo made a few attempts to move back to my side, but Liam told him firmly to stay. Moo sat but kept his eyes on me.

"I'll be around. See you soon."

I walked back to the conference room down the hall, holding the book Liam gave me, while settling into the warmth of being happy with my place in life. My hand instinctively reached out to pet Moo. He wasn't there, and I chuckled lightly at how used I'd become to that big, goofy beast.

Jess was gone, but someone else was in the conference room. He had his cheek and phone pressed up against the window while tapping on the phone. He was lanky and young. His clothes hung off him, especially his pants. He slid the phone up into the top corner of the window, exposing at least half of his boxer shorts from the waistband down. There was a pink splotch on his cheek from being pressed up against the cold window. His hair swirled around his head, his bangs starting at the right ear, crossing his forehead, and ending at his left ear. As the hair slipped into his eyes, he jerked his head to the left to clear his vision.

I leaned out back into the hallway but there was no sign of Jess. I started to cross the room, with my hand outstretched. "Hi, my—"

"What's the Wi-Fi password?" He turned to look at me.

I stopped, my hand outstretched awkwardly. "What?"

"I don't get reception in here. I need the Wi-Fi password." He stared at me through his bangs.

Annoyance welled up in my chest. My mouth started moving before my brain could stop it. "Listen here, young man, I'm not giving you anything until I know who you are and why you're here." Young man? I was thirty, not eighty.

He sighed dramatically and crossed the room while offering his hand. "Hi, my name is Indy, and I'm here to work at the Westmound Summit this weekend. Jess told me to wait in here. Now, can I please have the password?"

My lips puckered as though I'd sucked on a lemon. "I'm Di. Pick the temp router. The password is westmoundsummit, all lower case, one word."

He entered the code, head craned forward, and without looking up, wandered over to a conference table, pulled out a chair, and flopped down.

In an attempt to walk off my annoyance, I left the room and went down the hallway toward the archery entrance. Entering was a group of people led by Jess.

As they wiped their shoes free of snow on the heavy floor mats, I called out to my roommate, "How was the drive?"

Mary kicked off her snow boots and placed them in the growing row of shoes. From the shoe racks, she grabbed her athletic shoes and slipped them on. All the employees kept sets of shoes at the entrances; otherwise, we would track in too much snow and mud. "Not too bad. The freeways were pretty clean, but it looks like we are getting more snow soon."

Pushing past her were two people I recognized. Tiger, a handsome elite archer, spread his arms. "Di, come here and give me some loving." He gave me a warm hug and spun me around.

"Quit copping a feel and let me give Princess a hug."

Tiger put me down, but instead of walking over for a hug, I crossed my arms and glared at Minx. The strawberry blonde laughed even harder and wrapped me in a hug anyway.

"I love teasing you so much, Ms. Princess Di. You never should have let me know that you hated the nickname."

Last time Minx was here, she had decided that Princess or Princess Di should be my official archery nickname, and I've had trouble shaking it. She continued to squeeze me while rocking back and forth until I gave in and hugged her back.

Behind them, a tiny young girl with dark hair, eyes, and skin cast furtive glances around the group. "Did you fly in, as well?" I asked.

She clasped her hands in front of her, wringing and twisting them. When Tiger laughed loudly, she jumped with a gasp then spun around to identify the culprit. She turned back to me with wide eyes. "What?" she squeaked.

I wasn't sure what part of the question was confusing. "Did you fly in with Tiger and Minx?" I cast around the group for help.

Mary caught my look and stepped over to join us.

"No, Mouse lives in Cheyenne. We stopped at her house so she could follow us over. She's homeschooled and graduated early. She applied to be an OSA." Mary put a friendly hand on Mouse's shoulder, causing her to jump.

The OSA, on-site athletes, program would give athletes a place to live, food, and training in exchange for a light work schedule at the center. Applications had only been open a few weeks. Robbie, the center's director, had decided to invite several of the most promising applicants out to work at the Westmound Summit.

Mouse held out a delicate hand to me. "Hi, I'm Sabrina but everyone calls me Mouse. Is it true that someone was killed here last month?"

No wonder she was so jumpy. I put an arm around her shoulder. "Yes, but don't worry. You'll be fine."

Jess raised her voice. "Hey, we should have started setting up already. We don't even have a second to waste." She marched down the hallway toward the conference room.

At the far end of the hall, Liam, Moo, and Westmound's owner, Elizabeth, turned the corner. Elizabeth lived in Salt Lake City, where Westmound was based, but she came in a day early for the Westmound Summit. Liam and Moo passed by with a quick sniff from Moo and a nod of the chin from Liam.

Elizabeth greeted the group with a warm,

appraising smile then turned to Jess. "Do you think you could give me five minutes to talk?"

Jess pushed her curly hair back out of her face. "Absolutely." Turning to us, she said, "Go on down to the conference room."

I turned to ask Mary what she thought this was about, but Elizabeth's voice interrupted me. "Actually, I was hoping Mary and Di could join us. Perhaps we could use Di's office?"

We walked down to my office, where I unlocked the door. I offered Elizabeth my plush desk chair while Jess, Mary, and I grabbed the remaining chairs to face her.

"I just finished talking to Liam, and he had an excellent idea. I wanted to see if you ladies would be on board. If you are, we can bring in Orion, Westmound's marketing director, and get started after Di and Mary return from Christmas break."

We nodded along, eagerly leaning forward. I had no idea where Elizabeth was going, but I wanted to please her.

Elizabeth turned to Mary. "Liam said that you are shooting archery again. How are you feeling about it?"

"Wonderful. Di and I shoot together every day. I

was hoping to talk to Liam at some point… about…"

Elizabeth finished Mary's thought. "Do you mean equipment?"

Mary nodded.

"I'll let Liam know that you will be setting up a meeting."

Elizabeth turned her attention to Jess. "I've heard that you are working with both Mary and Di. How is that going?"

"Very well, we are very careful to make sure that it doesn't conflict with our work. We make sure—"

Elizabeth waved her off. "No, no, I'm not worried about that. Let me back up. This weekend, you will hear a lot more about this. Our goal is to broaden our customer base, and one of the largest areas of focus is women. Liam recommended that Di receive a Westmound sponsorship deal for equipment, Mary renew her contract, and then we document their progress on the website. Does that sound that like something we can do?"

Jess burst with excitement. "That would be wonderful. I could put together training schedules and maybe record some of the coaching sessions. Oh, we have that new form analysis room in development—we could use that some. It would really show off the center and the elite coaching available here."

Mary was close on her heels. She was perched on the edge of her seat, her eyes wide and eager. The words tumbled out of her mouth, one on top of the other. "I could try out a bunch of different equipment and talk about the differences. Talk about my tuning methods. I have charts and software I use to monitor the results that I could share. This is awesome."

Everyone turned to me waiting for my response. "Huh?" I realized that I should clarify more when three sets of eyes landed on me. "I wasn't asking Liam to get me free stuff. I would love to be involved, but I can pay for—"

Elizabeth stopped me before I could babble on further. "It isn't for free; therefore, don't worry about that. It would be in exchange for promoting our products and agreeing to train and document your journey so others getting into the sport can benefit from the knowledge. This isn't something you have to do just because you work at the center, but if you want to, then we would love to have you."

I looked at Mary and Jess, who were nodding at me. I still didn't fully understand what I was committing to, but if they thought it was a good idea, then I trusted them. I took a deep breath and blew it out slowly, feeling very Zen. "I'd be honored to be involved."

"Wonderful. I wish I had more time to discuss it, but I know you all have a lot to do. I will let Liam and Orion know what we discussed. I'll see you here at range day tomorrow."

Elizabeth stood up and headed out the hallway to the front entrance.

Jess was beside herself. "Isn't this so great? I can't believe it."

One thing had really stuck out to me. "She puts a lot of weight on Liam's opinion."

Mary turned to me with a puzzled expression. "Why wouldn't she trust her son?"

"Her son? He can't be her son. His name isn't Westmound. It's......" I searched around for his last name. "Andersson. Liam Andersson."

Jess turned to me with a giggle. "You dork. Her last name isn't Westmound, either, not since she got married. Her name is Elizabeth Andersson, like Andersson Archery, her husband's company before he passed. How did you not know this?"

I was flabbergasted. "I-I don't know. Oh geez, I'm

a huge idiot." I buried my face into my hands with embarrassment. My face was burning, and I didn't want them to see me blush.

Mary and Jess laughed while Mary gave my back a pat. "Hey, you're being too hard on yourself. You're probably only a little idiot." They both snorted a bit more.

I dropped my hand to roll my eyes at them.

Jess checked her watch again. "We are really behind. We have to get over to the meeting."

"Can I catch up in ten minutes? I'm supposed to keep Moo today. I need to pick him up with his stuff." And I could apologize to Liam.

"Ten minutes and not a second more," Jess called to me as I left the office.

CHAPTER TWO

I trotted to the entrance, slipped on my snow boots, and stepped outside to find Liam. I walked by a cop car parked in front of the building. Knocking on the window, I gave Brian, the officer in the front seat, playing games on his phone, a quick wave. He had been at the center when the previous killer had been apprehended, and had quickly become a center regular. This weekend, he was acting as security though I imagine he'll mostly be looking at the new product lines being introduced rather than checking badges at the door.

Liam and Moo were out in the field next to the parking lot, playing. There were several inches of snow already on the ground, and thick, heavy flakes slowly drifted to the ground. Thick gray clouds obscured the sky. I walked out into the field and waved to get Liam's attention. Moo caught sight of me and raced across the field. I stomped my feet and crouched to welcome him.

"No!"

I looked up to see Liam running across the field with a worried look.

I looked back to Moo, who was barreling toward me. I waited for him to dodge left or right to run past me, but at the last second, I realized he wasn't slowing down. The last thing I saw was his pink tongue and big brown eye bearing down on me before impact.

I hit the ground flat on my back. The snow puffed out around me, breaking my fall as I landed. Snow drifted down on my face, catching in my eyelashes. The back of my neck was cold and wet. I lay in the snow, my eyes closed, mentally checking over my arms and legs as Moo shoved his cold, wet nose into my shut eyes and pawed at my arm.

"No, bad, Moo," Liam said from somewhere above me.

Moo made an anguished moan at the correction and threw himself on top of me; his pointy elbows digging into my stomach and one of his front paws scratching my arm.

I tentatively opened an eye to see that Liam had grabbed Moo by the collar to pull him off. "Come on. Off! Off! Moo, now."

Moo resisted by flopping hard onto my chest, and a whoosh of air escaped my lungs. I reached up to pet him, and he finally moved to the ground next to me and gave me a lick from chin to hairline before racing off to grab a ball on the far side of the field.

"Are you okay? Did you hit your head?" Liam knelt beside me.

"I'm fine, just a bruised ego."

I felt a bit disoriented, but when Liam grabbed both my hands and pulled me up, right into his arms, the feeling shifted. After a few moments, he dropped my hand, but the impression of his grip stayed.

He started wiping snow off my back and legs. "I'm sorry, Di. I tried to warn you. Moo thinks that snow on the ground means it's okay to play rough. I only adopted him last spring, so I didn't realize until now. Do you need to go to your room and lay down?"

I stretched my neck back and forth a few times. "No, I'm fine. I was surprised more than anything. I need to get back to the meeting."

Liam trotted over to a bag on the ground, and I

followed. "This is all of Moo's stuff. Are you sure you're okay dogsitting him?"

I laughed and reached back to wipe at some snow stuck under the back of my collar. "What's a little mauling between friends?"

Liam whistled, and when Moo trotted over, he clipped a leash on Moo's collar. "You might want to keep him on a leash when you are outside until I get him trained. Thanks! I need to head over to the hotel."

He turned and headed toward his car. I suddenly remembered why I had been so eager to talk to him. "Hey, Liam."

He turned around. I shouted across the distance as I closed it. "I just found out that you're Elizabeth's son. Did you *know* that I didn't know?"

His clear laugh rang out across the parking lot as he smiled at me, the corners of his eyes crinkled with mirth. "Yes, I figured it out when you asked if I had known Mrs. Westmound long."

"Why didn't you tell me?"

"I wanted to see how long it would take to figure it out on your own, Ms. Detective. I'll see you tomorrow." He got into his truck and slowly exited the parking lot while Moo and I stood in the snow and waved.

Stepping back into the center, I changed out of my snow boots and wiped off the rest of the snow that was clinging to my arms, then I unclipped Moo, and we jogged down the hallway into the conference room. Tiger and Mouse were assembling bags with material on one table while Indy and Minx talked quietly, stuffing name tags into holders. Mary and Jess sat at another table, discussing a chart.

"Glad you could join us. Come over here so I can show you—what is wrong with your hair?" Jess said.

I patted my hair, finding a crusty spot where Moo had licked me. I did my best to flatten it, but when I was done, my hand smelled faintly of dog drool. I had missed some snow on the back of my legs, and it was melting through my pants to my skin. My back and neck ached a bit as the adrenaline wore off, but the prevailing sensation I noticed was my hand tingling from where Liam had helped me up. I rubbed the hand to remove the distraction.

"Moo and I had a little accident outside."

Jess nodded then pointed at a diagram. "Everyone has their assignments already. Your work is easy. We will sit at the Westmound Center table at this side of the room and stay there. Mary will be with you most of the time and the rest of the volunteers when they don't have an active assignment. I'm going to have meetings with anyone that is interested in setting up a workshop or camp at the center; you'll keep a copy of the schedule at your table. I basically want you to be our headquarters. If someone needs something, you can provide it. Is that clear enough?"

"Aye, aye, Captain." I gave her a formal salute, but she wasn't looking at me. Mary snorted at my failed joke, and I stuck my tongue out at her.

Jess picked up a roll of tape and a stack of index cards with large numbers on them. "Come on. We need to go tape these markers on the range floor."

Mary and I followed Jess across the hall to the large indoor archery range. It was the size of a football field and allowed archers to practice the outdoor distances year-round under ideal conditions: no rain, no wind, and no excuses.

Jess handed Mary and me each a stack of cards, a roll of flooring-safe tape, and a diagram.

The diagram covered the entire range.

"Are these all companies owned by Westmound?"

Mary said, "Yes," right as Jess said, "No."

After a chuckle, Jess clarified, "Yes, Westmound

owns all these, but not all these labels are individual companies. For instance, Andersson Archery gets three spots: one for the competitive recurve bow line, one for the competitive compound line, and one for the hunting line of bows. Many of the larger companies will get several spots."

I pushed an errant strand of hair behind my ear. "I can't believe how big this summit is."

Mary spun around from where she was taping down a label. Her face was shining with excitement. "If you think this is big, you should see the Outdoor Industry Trade Show next month. The OIT Show is huge. Over a hundred thousand people from all over the world attend. I want to go back so badly."

Jess smiled smugly. "Robbie and I are going to the OIT show to represent the center, and we get to celebrate our anniversary while we are there."

***

"We open in fifteen minutes! I needed you here much earlier." Jess had been up long before us. She spotted us standing in the doorway and rushed over.

"You told us to come at this time." I double-checked my phone. We had stayed up late last night watching TV in our room while I started reading the book Liam had given me.

Jess's coffee breath tickled my nose. Her normally wild, curly hair was held back in a chignon, but out of habit she tucked a non-existent strand of hair behind her ear. "But you should have known I would need you earlier, regardless of what time we agreed on."

Mary, Mouse, Indy, Minx, Tiger, Moo, and I had already grabbed breakfast together, and were ready to work, but after rooming with Jess for four years in college, being friends for over a decade, and working together for the past two months, I had to admit she was right. I should have predicted her last-minute freak-out. "You're right, but we're here now. What do you need?"

"Minx and Indy, can you put up these signs? Here's a map—I noted where each sign goes. Tiger and Mouse, head over to check-in with Bruce. The buses from the hotel should be arriving any minute. Mary and Di, go to man the center's table. Once your job is done, go to the center's table so Di can send you out on your next job. Di, do you have the tablets?" Jess started to look more relaxed as she bossed us around.

"Yes, I grabbed them from my office this morning. The ones assigned to the ranges are there already. The rest will be with me." I handed Jess her tablet. I had put together a system so each person in the system could hit a button indicating where they were, what they were doing or if they needed help. I hoped it would simplify communication between the center staff.

Mary and I headed to the far wall, where the seventy-meter target mats normally stood. I was awed by all the different exhibits. Most had colorful walls of advertising, many had set up their own cushioned flooring, and some even had tables and chairs.

Moo's freedom was restricted today, with all the people and activity. He was in his harness with a leash, but I had put a Christmas sweatshirt over the top of it. The arms were chopped off to not interfere with his walking, and there was a hole for the leash to attach to the harness. I settled him onto his bed between the tables, in front of the huge Westmound Center display panel. He circled three times, lay down, and set to work trying to bite the harness. The nylon straps were just beyond the reach of his teeth, but that didn't prevent him from trying over and over before flopping onto his other side and trying again. I reached over and scratched his ears until he settled in and fell asleep.

The room was filling with people moving to their

tables. The opening speech was supposed to be soon, then we could start doing whatever it was we were supposed to do on range day of the Westmound Summit.

I turned to Mary. "Have you been to one of these before?"

Mary dragged her attention back to me, "Yeah. Two years ago, I went to write up articles for Westmound to send out to employees that were unable to attend the event. Last year, though, I couldn't attend, and they hired Cold to film it instead."

"What exactly happens today? I mean, I know that this is a brand summit for Westmound. They want consistency within the entire brand along with all the companies having a basic understanding of new products, but why have everyone come to one location? Couldn't they just send out an e-mail?"

"It's much more than that. They have a party, give out bonuses and awards for performance and general information, but that's the next few days at the hotel conference. Today is range day: it is all about playing with the new products, networking, and shooting."

I thought about it for a second, but it still felt like I was missing some angle. "So they all get together to shoot?"

Mary laughed. "I bet they would; people in this industry really love what they do. Let me give you a better example. Andersson Archery has a new entry-level competitive recurve bow. So someone from there might go over to Bucky Sights, Knight Products and Quaker Stabilizers and put together a solid entry level competition bow from all Westmound products. Then go to the short range that Bruce is running to see how it shoots. Then they can market it together as a ready-to-shoot setup." Mary pointed to each company in turn. "Then at the OIT show next month, they can have literature available and push the full setup with a slight discount to archery pro-shops putting in orders. That's just an archery example, but something similar is happening for handguns, shot guns, rifles, *et cetera.*"

"So one big happy family helping each other sell more products?" I asked.

"Basically. Didn't they explain this in all the director meetings you attend every week?"

Jess had snuck up on us without me noticing. "Di basically sleeps through those."

"I do not."

"This is Di every meeting." Jess stared off into the

distance, her mouth hanging open and her eyes wide and empty.

"Shut up. You're such a pill." I looked around for something to throw at her.

"Right, Liam? This is totally Di in the weekly meetings."

I turned around to see Liam chuckling behind me at Jess's impression. "Hey, you guys are supposed to be my friends and be on my side!"

Liam gave my shoulder a squeeze. "We are. Tablet?"

I handed him his tablet and smiled back.

Jess laughed. "I'm just giving you a hard time. Everyone knows that if they need something from you, they just need to get your attention and tell you exactly what they need then, bam! —like, two hours later, they'll have it. Your daydreaming isn't an issue because you're so dang good at your job."

Approaching from behind Liam was an athletic-looking, thirty-something, handsome black man. He had posture that radiated that he was in charge. He stopped as Liam asked us another question. "Has anyone seen Orion yet?"

The man behind Liam answered, "Everyone but

you."

Liam swung around and grabbed the man's hand to shake before they hugged. They clapped each on the back repeatedly before breaking apart. Liam introduced Orion to everyone with, "This is Orion, the marketing director for Westmound and one of my oldest friends."

With an easy smile, Orion said, "Easy with that 'old' business. I'm not getting older, only better."

Orion greeted me with a handshake. "Di, it's nice to meet the new computer expert," he said before turning to shaking Mary's hand with, "Nice to see you back at the Westmound Summit, Mary." He moved down to Jess with a, "You're doing a great job with the center's archery program, Jess," then he turned back to Liam. "I can see why you extended your sabbatical. You have a great facility and team here. We may never convince you to return to headquarters."

Liam and Orion were so similar that it wasn't surprising they were close friends. They were dressed not just in the same Westmound polo but jeans with a similar loose-cut, flat-bottom shoes and even slightly similar haircuts. Orion seemed to read all of Liam's subtle nods with perfect accuracy. "Liam's right; we need to get going."

As they walked off in unison, they slowed down often to shake hands. Orion greeted everyone by name and asked after a spouse, child, or hobby.

"Oh crap, I forgot what I came over here for." Jess pulled out a huge ring of keys. "Can you unlock the door over here then go unlock the bathrooms on this side of the range? Lock the rest of the doors, please. Here, Mary, can you hang this sign? Please, hurry. Liam and Orion are supposed to do the introduction any minute."

Jess disappeared after putting the keys and a sign marked Bathroom on our table. I woke up Moo and dragged him along. I unlocked the door and propped it open while Mary affixed the sign. This door was kept locked because the last thing we needed was someone wandering into the range from behind the target.

The whole section was empty for now. Hopefully, over time, it would become an area bustling with offices and programs. I walked through the empty room and out another door in the far end of the hallway, then I turned right and headed down toward the bathrooms.

Checking that each door was locked, I passed a future lounge. A bank of windows looked into the hallway, and another bank of windows on the far wall looked out into Wyoming winter. I was surprised to see that snow was falling steadily from a gray sky.

The weather report said a storm was coming to Wyoming, but they had thought it would swing much farther north. Perhaps not. I checked that the doorway between this hall and the main hallway was locked. There was an offshoot to the right, and I turned down the short hall. There were three large bathrooms. I unlocked them and checked that they were clean and that the light worked.

These bathrooms were built to accommodate athletes in wheelchairs, families with children, or crowds at times like this when more bathrooms were needed.

The only other room was a storage room where the center was storing the couches. I checked that the door was locked, finishing up everything that Jess requested, as I turned back into the main hallway. In the far-upper corner was the recently installed video surveillance camera. I gave it a friendly wave even though I knew no one was watching. All the footage was automatically uploaded to a cloud server. It was a bit like closing the barn door after the horses were out, but it would be stupid not to install surveillance after the murder. Hopefully, we would never need it.

When I stepped back into long range, Orion was on a small stage up front, talking to everyone as they crowded around.

CHAPTER THREE

I snuck over to Mary, dragging Moo behind me as he strained to say hi to all the people. Orion was quite visible from my table. I leaned in close to Mary. "What did I miss?"

"He's trying to convince them to get excited about the idea of advertising to new demographics. It might be a hard sell."

I pulled Moo in close for scratches. "What does 'new demographics' mean?"

"Someone other than white males."

I mouthed, "Oh," and tuned into Orion's speech.

"...love more than anything else on earth? That's right—other people passionate about the shooting sports. So let's bring more people, and their money, into our industry."

A hardy chuckle and a round of applause went up at the word *money*. Orion had a flare for working the room.

"Let me give you an example of one project. The fastest growing demographic in shooting sports is women. We're seeing huge increases across the board except the numbers aren't growing as fast in archery. The Westmound Center is looking to launch a new campaign soon to help introduce more women in archery. Are Di and Mary around here somewhere?"

Mary leaped out of her seat and started waving until she caught Orion's eye. Once he saw us, he waved and motioned for us to stand up. Heads started turning.

"Mary and Di are employees of the center and archers. Many of you may already know Bloody Mary from her aggressive shooting style that dominated youth archery. As she transitions into adult archery, she will work with Westmound to show the public her training schedule, how she picks out equipment and anything else on her mind. Di, on the other hand, used to be an archer in......help me out, Di."

I lifted my voice to carry over the crowd. "End of high school and all through college."

"Right. But now she is coming back into the sport

as an adult. She is very much in line with what we see from competitive female archers: educated, competitive women with highly demanding jobs. Who wouldn't want that kind of customer?"

A man in the crowd yelled out, "Customer? That's the kind of gal I want to marry," to a boom of laughter.

I leaned over Mary. "Is that true?"

"It's pretty true. We have a lot of moms and archery coaches that compete but at my last tournament, I shot on a target with three lawyers. On the right were three engineers, and on the left was a surgeon."

I had no idea. I focused back on Orion, hoping that I hadn't missed much. "…an example of an authentic way to promote the sport. But we have two more days to listen to me talk. For now, let's go shoot!"

The crowd gave a cheer and drifted back across the range to start the process of having fun.

Orion pushed through the crowd to our table.

"I hope you didn't mind me putting you on the spot," he said.

We shook our heads, and I added, "Not at all."

"Good, I think it sounds like a great idea." He shook a few hands as people walked by, but he didn't attempt to leave our table.

"It's hardly that unique," I said.

"For archery, it is. Most of these companies are using the same marketing strategy they have had for the past several decades. I'm trying to get them excited about new opportunities. I have my first meeting in a few minutes, but we'll talk about your ideas soon." He gave us a dazzling smile before leaving.

Mouse and Tiger passed Orion, who introduced himself, and approached the table. Mouse sat next to Moo on his bed and petted him.

"Uh, you okay down there? I can get you a chair." I didn't want to be a bad host.

"It's okay; I love dogs." She cooed softly to Moo, speaking quietly. His eyes rolled back in his head, his tongue lolled out, and he flopped across her lap.

Tiger stared intently at the MacSights booth a few dozen yards away. One panel of the display was named Kandi-covered, with a stunning bottle blonde and more bosoms than could possibly have been bestowed by genetics alone. The image was twice the size of real life, and her cleavage looked big enough to sleep in. Nestled between the breasts was a tiny tattoo of a pink-and-white lollypop, and a tagline on the wall proclaimed,

"Everything is better when it's Kandi-covered." A variety of archery equipment in bright pink surrounded the perimeter. Underneath was *Kandi* scrawled in a flowing signature with a heart dotting the *i*. A bouncy blonde matching the sign stood in the booth, her cleavage overflowing, in weather-inappropriate shorts that skimmed her butt cheeks.

Tiger drifted away from the table. "How about if I check if anyone needs anything?"

We watched him approach the blonde, who squealed and threw a hug around his neck. He closed his eyes, and a smile overtook his face as she bounced against him.

Mary huffed beside me. "Ugh, I can't believe she is dressed like that."

Being older than Mary, I wanted to set a mature example. "It really isn't our business how she dresses."

"So you would dress that way?"

"Uh no. What does the back of her shirt say?" I leaned over the table hoping that being a foot closer would help me read it. "It's not a party until you take Kandi and liquor. Ewww."

Mary leaned back in her seat. "I don't get why it's gross."

"It's a pun, liquor and 'lick her.' She is saying people should lick her. Nevermind" I didn't want to get into a drawn-out discussion critiquing another person's looks, even if she was tacky.

"MacSights is a pretty popular brand, though they don't make recurve sights, only compound ones. I didn't realize they were bought out by Westmound."

A gruff voice interrupted our conversation. "I see that the Westmound Center has a thing for hiring a bunch of chicks."

The speaker was a man holding a camera and standing next to a large tripod. He had an aggressively masculine face that overshot handsome and landed in severe. He probably lived in the gym. In theory, that should have made him fit, but instead, it repelled me. Combined with his opening line, I was finding him less than attractive.

He stood there, smiling down at us. "Hey, Mary, good to see you are still around. Do you still write those little articles?"

Mary bristled next to me and snapped back, "They aren't 'little articles.' They're for the leading online archery publication in the world. I don't write them as often as I used to since I started college."

He held his hands up. "Don't get so emotional; I was only asking. No one reads anymore, so I wasn't sure. If you ever have any questions about how real journalism is done now, just let me know."

Mary pursed her mouth.

Thinking things might get out of hand, I shoved my verbal foot in the door. "Hi, I'm Di. And you are?" I extended my hand.

He grabbed my hand and attempted to crush my fingers in his grip. "I'm Cold of Cold Hard Facts, the leader in Archery video journalism. I'm sure you know my work."

I politely nodded and did my best to retrieve my hand without tearing it out of his grasp. "What can we do for you?"

Cold moved the tripod in front of the table and started to attach the camera on top. "I need to get a quick summary for the video I am doing on the Westmound Summit." Pulling a microphone out of his back pocket, he handed it to me. "Just give me a second to get set up. Why don't you girls figure out what you are going to say?" He looked closely at my face then over at Mary with a grimace. "You might want to put on some lipstick or makeup."

I turned to Mary with my best can-you-believe-this-guy look, but she was glaring at him already. Suddenly, her jaw dropped, and she burst out of her chair. "Holy schnikeys!"

I turned in the direction she was staring to see that Minx was in the MacSights booth, having a heated argument with Kandi. Their voices carried but were not clear enough to make out. Indy and Tony stood behind Minx, watching Kandi and Minx as they yelled back and forth.

Suddenly, Kandi leaned forward and shoved Minx hard. Minx stumbled backward. I sucked in my breath but before I could move Minx lifted an arm and with the full force of her body slapped Kandi. The room went quiet a second before the crack of skin on skin rang out clearly. Kandi's whole body shuddered. In the stillness, two more voices rose in conflict. A large man with a pale, sweaty face was poking his finger into the chest of a thinner man. Before I could see much more, the crowd descended and broke them apart.

Orion and Jess pulled about a dozen people from the room. As they left the range, conversations exploded all around us.

"I got that on camera." Cold pushed buttons on

the side of his camera.

I swung back to look at Cold and felt uneasy. He seemed far too pleased and smug.

"Give me the memory card." I extended my hand, palm up.

His head turned to me. "No way."

"According to your contract, all footage shot on the premise of the Westmound Center belongs to Westmound. So hand it over."

Somewhere during those daydreaming meetings, I had managed to capture this single fact. Jess had mentioned that she had heard some unsavory rumors about Cold. Liam had countered that they had a great contract written, and he was willing to give him one last chance.

"She's right." I didn't even have to turn around to know the Liam had come up behind me.

Cold looked at me then Liam. He took the memory card out of the camera, slammed it down on the table, then grabbed his camera and left. I slipped it into my pocket and turned to Liam.

"Thanks for the backup. He caught that whole fight on camera and seems a bit too smug about it. That is not the kinda thing we want all over the Internet."

"Smart. Anything else?"

When I shook my head, Liam left.

Turning back to Mary, I asked, "Is it always this exciting? Should we get some riot gear?"

"That was crazy. I was right there. I am pretty sure Minx could have taken Kandi, but it was really close." Indy was sitting on the other side of Moo. "You know, my dad dated both of them."

"So did my dad," said a male voice from behind me.

A guy in his twenties had come up to the table and joined the conversation. He half turned to hook his thumb over his shoulder at the MacSights booth. He was wearing jeans with the back pockets covered in rhinestones and metal rivets. They were held up by a leather belt with a belt buckle bigger than my hand.

"And who is your dad?"

"Mac of MacSights. Big guy. Married to Kandi. You can call me M.C., marketing director of MacSights."

Introductions went around the group while he sat on the corner of the table. He seemed to be around Kandi's age if her promotional picture on the panel was anything to go by. "Kandi's your step-mom?"

He laughed. "She would have a fit if you called her that."

I thought about the two men fighting after Minx had hit Kandi—the bigger one was wearing the same red polo that M.C. had on. "Was your dad the gentleman in the fight? What was that about?"

"Yes, that was my dad. Who knows what started it this time? He is a racist, sexist bigot and isn't scared to share it."

We all exchanged looks. I was thrown off by his casual attitude. "Is that a joke or…?"

He laughed. "It's okay. He pretty much hates everyone equally, and they hate him."

The large-set man from the earlier fight approached our table. As he drew close, I saw that the skin on his face hung loosely, as though he had recently lost a lot of weight. His pale, moist skin was even more unsettling up close. His pallor was sickly. Dark circles under his eyes sunk into the sockets under his eyes as he mopped at his face with a handkerchief. He looked at Mary and bellowed, "Are you Di?"

Mary pointed to me, and I picked up the conversation. "I'm Di. Can I help you with something?"

He wiped his forehead again. "After all that

excitement, I think I need to lie down. This altitude is getting to me. Plus, I think I picked up the flu. Jess said you could show me a room with a couch."

I grabbed the keys and Moo; I could take him outside to potty after I got Mac settled in. I gestured for him to follow me. I tried to engage in polite chatter as I walked him to the room next to the bathrooms. I suspected that Bruce, the archery coach at the center focused on community outreach and beginning instructions, snuck in there in the afternoon to take a nap on the couches. His hair was often flattened in the late afternoons.

"How are you enjoying the summit so far?" I asked as we headed down the long hallway.

"I'm sure it's great for others, but I've built this company from the ground up and don't need no n—" He cut himself off with a dry cough. "Boy telling me to market my sights to chicks and minorities. They don't buy bows. Boyfriends and husbands buy bows for their girlfriends and wives. That's who you advertise to. And the rest don't buy bows, and we don't need them to, either."

I stumbled in shock. "Uh, I'm a woman, and I planned on buying my own equipment. Mary is a

Korean female, and she picks out her own equipment."

"Oh, come on, sweetheart, Westmound will give you and that Asian chick stuff because you're pretty and sex sells. And the Asian is practically white, so she doesn't count. Maybe get some lower-cut shirts, though. You should talk to Kandi—she knows how to use her strengths to move product."

I unlocked the door and pushed it open. I didn't trust my voice to talk without chewing him out. At my previous job, a tech company I ran, no one would have dared to speak to me that way. Clients and employees respected me and treated me as the equal I was, even when they disagreed. Mac was talking to me like a child, and it set everything in me to boiling.

He passed me and slapped my butt. "If you get bored, feel free to come back. I can give you some private lessons."

He closed the door before I could explode.

Moo let out a bark and leaped at the door but bounced back onto his butt. He settled for a long, low growl. I pulled him away and scratched behind his ears as we walked, but I didn't correct him.

CHAPTER FOUR

We spent a few minutes outside, attending to dog business. The snow fell steadily, and the dry snowdrifts were building at a rapid pace. I kept Moo on his leash, and he raced back and forth as far as it would reach, hopping and bouncing, snapping at snowflakes as they fell.

I tried to push away my frustrations with my conversation with Mac. There was a time when I wouldn't have been affected by his remarks, but this time, they had gotten under my skin. Maybe I was still reeling from getting a divorce, or maybe it was the lack of confidence that comes with a heading in a new direction, but regardless, I needed to work harder on not letting the opinions of others affect me when I knew they were wrong.

After going back into the center, I wiped the snow off us both and took Moo to say hi to Brian.

"Hey Brian. You enjoying the summit?"

"I can't see much from here." His shoulders sagged forward, and the corners of his mouth pulled down as he looked over his shoulder at the exhibits visible through the range windows.

I checked around; the parking lot out front was still, and the buses that had brought everyone over in the morning were gone. "I bet it would be okay if you walked around for a bit. Just keep one eye on the door in case anyone shows up." He was supposed to be security and check that everyone coming in had a proper name tag, but the range had enough windows that he could move around and still keep an eye on the door. Plus, what was the likelihood that someone would show up now?

He sprang out of his chair. "Really? I could totally do that. If anyone asks, I can tell them that you said I could?" He waited to hear my reply.

I chuckled since I knew that the anyone he was referring to was Jess. Range day was her event at the Westmount Summit, and she had put the fear of God into all of us at the idea of letting it be ruined.

"Perfect. In fact, I'll message her and tell her that I suggested your appearance on the floor was a good idea so people were aware there was security on site."

Brian turned and started jogging down the hallways before stopping. "You might want to mention the snow to her. I have been listening, and the interstate is already having a problem with accidents. Officers are helping stranded motorists. If this snow keeps up, you might consider getting the buses out early; otherwise, everyone might be stuck here overnight."

"Thanks, I'll let her know." Right after I donned my fireproof panties. Jess was going to have a cow at the idea of her perfect day being ruined, but having all these people stuck here overnight would be even worse. I grabbed my phone and wrote out a quick message as I walked down the hallway to the range entrance.

Making it across the range was a slow process, people wanted to meet Moo, and sometimes, they even said hi to me, as well. I was embarrassed to admit that I recognized few of the company names and none of the people. I would need to spend some time during my Christmas break studying so this didn't happen again. If something was worth doing, it was worth overdoing and being completely obsessed about. I vowed that by the time I returned in the New Year, I would have memorized every company owned by Westmound.

Mary sat at the Westmound table alone.

"Where'd everyone go?"

"Tiger, Mouse, and Indy went to the kitchen. The staff is baking Christmas cookies and asked if we could pass them out. Look what I found in the bathroom." She held out a phone to me.

"Do you know who it belongs to?" She shook her head. "Let's just see what it says." I unlocked the phone since there was no password required and instantly got an eyeful.

"Are those breasts?" Mary leaned over close to the phone. "Yep, those are breasts, a hand squeezing one and a pink lollypop tattoo."

I clicked the phone to lock it again. We both looked at the MacSights booth and Kandi's visible lollypop tattoo. "Kandi's breasts, tattoo, and a man's hand. I think we have seen enough. It must be Mac's phone." I put it facedown on the table and pushed it away with my fingertip. I couldn't stand the thought of it being too close to me. "We'll give it back when he wakes up."

I reached into my bag of supplies, pulled out hand

sanitizer, then passed it to Mary with a shudder.

Minx stomped back to our table, her eyes rimmed red and puffy, and flopped down into a chair.

"Minx, what happen—" I started to ask.

"Nothing, I don't want to talk about it." She slumped farther in her seat.

"Indy and M.C. said—"

"I do *not* want to talk, at all." She sniffled hard.

It looked like she was ready to cry again. I dug a tissue out of my bag of supplies and passed it to Mary to pass to Minx.

A man without a name tag approached the table. He was the epitome of the good looking boy next door if the boy next door had zero body fat. The only thing that ruined his good looks was the scowl hardening his face.

"Where's the person in charge?" he snapped.

Minx and Mary both hooked a thumb at me.

I sighed. "How can I help you?"

"No, I need the person really in charge." He looked around for someone more important.

Minx burst out of her seat. "Don't you talk to her like that. That's Di and she *is* in charge." I was startled by Minx's slightly misplaced support. Jess had put me in charge while everyone else was in meetings and enjoying range day, but my power was minimal.

He continued to look around, the scowl still in place. "That's not what I meant. I need someone from Westmound. Is Elizabeth around?"

Minx slapped her hand on the table. "So typical—you think cause you're some hot shot archer that you can treat everyone else like crap, and that's not right." On the last word, her voice cracked. Whatever had upset her probably had little to do with the guy in front of us. A tear spilled from her eyes, and with a gasp, she ran from the table and headed toward the back bathrooms through the nearby door.

The guy scrubbed his face with his hand, and the scowl disappeared as he watched her race away. "I'm sorry. It's been a rough week. Is she going to be okay?"

"Yes, she is having a tough day, as well."

"Really, I'm serious. I'm sorry." He looked contrite, like a little boy if little boys were about six and a half feet tall.

I stood up and extended my hand. "Let's just start over. I'm Di, and this is Mary."

He shook my hand then reached for Mary. "I'm Loggin. Nice to meet you, Di. Mary, have we met before? Maybe at a 3D tournament?"

Mary shook her head. "No, I shoot recurve. But I think we could have met at Vegas?"

"Yes, it was the Vegas tournament, maybe three years ago."

"Tell Di that I'm normally a very likable guy." He turned to me with a crooked smile.

Mary turned to me. "Loggin is normally a very nice guy."

I chuckled. "Now, what can I do to help you?"

A pained look crossed his face, and the smile fell away. "I still need to talk to Elizabeth, unless you can correct a missed sponsorship payment?"

Orion came hustling up to the table "Is there a problem here?" He looked between Loggin and us, casually moving between us.

Loggin stepped back from the talk and turned to Orion. "I really need to talk to someone right away."

Orion shook Loggin's hand and asked me over his shoulder, "Di, can you use your tablet to add Loggin to my meeting schedule? There's an opening this afternoon." He turned back to Loggin. "I have a few minutes right now. Why don't I walk you over the dining area, and we can talk on the way."

Right after Orion and Loggin left, Liam came jogging up. "I heard there was a problem. Are you okay, Di?"

I waved him off with a big smile. "Don't worry; Orion took care of it. He's been great today."

Liam stared at me for a few seconds. "Yeah," he said then left.

I turned to Mary, throwing my hand up in the air in frustration. "Why is everyone acting so weird today?"

***

The rest of the day raced on. We directed people to the bathrooms, started a list of missing items including some t-shirts and a large knife, and sent Indy, Mouse and Tiger around to pass out a metric ton of Christmas cookies. Indy followed Mouse from booth to booth defeating the purpose of giving them both a tray of cookies. Tiger only visited the booths where woman were and stayed too long at each booth. Minx hid in the bathroom for quite a while. When she returned she slid behind our table and sulked.

The snow continued to fall and the decision was made to call the buses back early for fear that everyone would be stranded over night at the center. Moo had been antsy for the past hour; he was used to a busy day of following me around the center. I tried to entertain him with a rousing game of tug-of-war but he didn't even attempt to win.

M.C. came over to the table from the MacSight booth where Kandi was hovering. "We need to get packed up. Where's my dad?"

I had forgotten about him. "I'll grab him."

I snagged Moo, and we jogged to the doorway. I held the leash loosely and once we were in the hallway, he started pulling hard on the leash. "Hey, Moo, ease up a little."

He barked and sniffed the air. The little hairs on his scruff raised and I was uneasy. Mac had been taking a nap for an awfully long time.

We rounded the corner. Moo strained hard to reach the closed door, sniffing all along the perimeter of the door before he started pawing at it, scratching off flakes of paint.

Tentatively, I turned the handle and wedged myself between Moo and the door. I was overwhelmed with the metallic smell of blood. It reminded me of every nosebleed and bit cheek I'd ever had. I slammed the door shut. My heart pounded in my chest. My stomach clenched and twisted.

"Not again."

CHAPTER FIVE

I didn't know what to do. What if Mac was just hurt and I needed to get in there and help him? I reached for the door but couldn't bring myself to touch the handle. Moo whined and wedged his nose into the crack at the bottom of the door. I messaged Mary to grab Brian and come to the bathrooms and not to say anything to anyone. She typed back a simple K immediately.

I checked that the bathrooms were empty, then Moo and I moved to the long hallways to wait. I tried to convince myself that I was overreacting, that everything was okay, and we would have a good laugh over the whole thing. Jess would tell me that I was trying to ruin her event but would say it with good humor, Mary would tell me that it could happen to anyone, and Liam would shake his head at my reaction.

Brian came trotting down the hallway with Mary in tow. "What's up?"

I should have thought of what to say. I wanted to blurt out that I smelled blood and Mac was dead, but if I was wrong I would be an idiot since I hadn't turned on the light to even look. I should have just looked myself. I pointed at the door and didn't say anything. He could figure it out on his own.

He opened the door and flipped on the light. I could hear him gasp and race into the room.

Mary took a step to follow him, and I grabbed her arm and shook my head. From where we stood, I couldn't see the interior of the room and thought it should stay that way.

Brian came back. "Did you touch anything?"

I shook my head. "I opened the door just an inch and could smell the blood. I didn't turn on the light. Is he…?"

He nodded his head, looking more serious than I had seen him since the last murder. "I should have known this wouldn't be an easy assignment. You installed video surveillance right? I need to see it right now. I already requested more officers, but the department is pretty spread thin with this weather."

"What's wrong with Mac?" Mary asked. I had forgotten about her. Her eyes were wide, and she shifted her weight between her feet uneasily.

"He was murdered," Brian said bluntly but gently. He watched her face and stood by until she nodded, then he talked into the unit on his shoulder.

I pulled Mary aside. "Are you okay? I know it can be a shock."

She shook her head.

Orion came down the hallway. "Is everything okay? Can I help?"

"Yes, you can." Brian stepped forward. "No one can leave yet. Can you do that?"

Orion nodded. "Sure thing." He jogged off and passed Liam in the hallway.

Liam came up, placed a hand on my shoulder, and leaned over to whisper, "What's wrong?"

I turned to him with a frown. "Mac was killed. Orion is making sure no one leaves."

Everything I said today seemed to annoy Liam. His eyes narrowed slightly, and he removed his hand from my shoulder.

Brian interrupted us before I could ask what was

wrong. "Di, can you lock up this area and show me the surveillance footage? No officer can come out here yet because there's a huge accident on the interstate. I need to start the investigation."

Brian sent Liam out somewhere while Mary and I followed him to the office, locking the doors as we left. In my office, I pulled up the footage of the hallway. Mary and Brian hovered behind me as we watched the sped up footage of me coming down the hallway and opening the bathroom, then we checked that everyone who went down the hallway returned. When we got to the footage of Moo and me escorting Mac down the hallway, I played the footage at normal speed.

"Brian, are we looking for anything in particular?"

"Let's see it once, and then I will tell you."

It turned out that while the door to the room wasn't visible, Moo was. I could see Moo's tail wagging through the thirty seconds it took me to open the door for Mac and return into view.

We raced through the rest of the footage. Brian carefully noted the timecode when someone disappeared from view into the short hallway and returned. When Moo and I appeared on camera to check on Mac, I was surprised to see that I only spent a few seconds out of sight at the doorway before reappearing on camera. I thought I had stood at the doorway forever, trying to work up the guts to turn on the light and see why I smelled so much blood. A pang of guilt ran through me——Mac had suffered some tragedy, and I was too chicken to even look. Maybe one dead body in a lifetime was all I could handle.

"Should I have gone into the room? Is there something I could have done to help him?" I wanted Brian to tell me that I had done the right thing.

"No, you should not have gone in there. You made the right choice."

"What happened to him?" Mary asked.

"You don't need to know that. I know that last time you two did an impression of Miss Marple and Columbo but this time—"

I cut him off. "Wait, which one am I? The old lady or the one with a bad eye?"

Brian didn't laugh. "I'm serious. You cannot look at video surveillance again, and you cannot go back to the crime scene. Tell me that you understand."

Mary and I exchanged a glance.

"If you find anything, you need to give it to me right away. And lastly, I cannot *see* you investigating.

Got it? If I *see* you investigating, I will stop you. I don't want to *see* you talking to suspects. I don't want to *see* you gathering evidence. I don't want to *see* any of that. I'm not just saying this as a cop but as your friend. Please."

"Of course, we've got it. We're not suspects, are we?"

"Not really. Neither of you were in there long enough, but in the meantime, don't go anywhere."

I turned to my left to look at Moo. I had gotten used to his constant presence. "Good to know we aren't suspects."

"I need to go grab everyone on the list, release the rest, and start this investigation." Brian left the room.

Mary flopped into a chair after snatching a pen and pad of paper off my desk.

Moo walked up behind Mary and looked over her shoulder at the notepad. When the pen slipped out of her grasp, he ducked down to pick it up, chewing on the end. He rested his head on her shoulder, pulling her off to the right. She straightened up, snatched the pen out of his mouth, and started writing a list of names while Moo watched.

"Here's our suspects. Are you ready to

investigate?"

Startled, I looked at her. "What? Weren't you listening? Brian doesn't want us to investigate."

Mary rolled her eyes at me. "How can someone so smart be so dense? He didn't say not to investigate. He said he didn't want to *see* us investigating."

"Is that why he kept saying *see, see, see*? I guess finding another body has really thrown me for a loop."

Mary put her feet on my desk. "It's a good thing you have me around to keep you in line."

I leaned over and waggled one of her feet. "You know what? You're right." I was lucky to have her in my life. She was determined and organized but still fun. She kept me in line and had been the roommate I'd never known I'd needed in my life. "Did you write down everyone from the video? Is the dynamic duo ready to ride again?" Last time we investigated, we'd had a running joke about being Batman and Robin.

Minx knocked on the open doorway, with Tiger at her side, a plate of cookies in her hand.

"This time, we get to help investigate," Minx said.

They came in and pulled up chairs. Moo trotted over to accept ear scratches from each.

Minx knocked Mary's feet off the desk and placed

the cookies on the corner of my desk. Mary reached out and grabbed a tree-shaped cookie before replying, "Tiger can investigate; he's the only one of us that never showed up in the footage at all."

He ruffled the side of Moo's neck with his knuckles. "I was busy. Orion's speech about women in the industry motivated me to talk to some people about an idea that I've had for a long time. If I get chosen to train here, I want to start a program where local women can come and learn all about firearms and archery in a female-only environment. I was talking to some companies to see if I could get their backing for the idea."

Minx snorted. "Whatever, you just wanted to flirt with women."

Tiger snapped back, "Treating women like intelligent peers and wanting to date them are not mutually exclusive ideas. I was raised by a single mother and have three younger sisters. Women are every bit as capable of doing things that I do, but when I was a kid and we went places, we were treated differently. We all shot guns and bows growing up. When I asked people how things worked, they would explain in detail, but when my sisters asked, they would be told not to worry about that stuff. I don't know why people think it is such a radical idea that women are people, too."

We all sat in silence for a moment. He had given his little speech with more than a bit of frustration. I admitted to thinking of him as only a flirt, but I realized that he had actually never been demeaning or dismissive of me.

Mary was looking at him with a huge smile. "That's a great idea. You want to teach?"

"Nah, that would kinda defeat the purpose. I want to have women teach the course, but I could do all the boring administrative stuff behind the scenes. Maybe if I'm lucky, though, they'll let me join the ladies for a meal or two. Show them what a gentleman I am." He waggled his eyebrows at her.

I laughed. "You're a complicated man, Tiger."

"All the best are." He reached over and broke a corner off a cookie. Flinging it into the air, he caught it in his mouth then ate it with a smug smile.

"Now that Tiger has enlightened us on his social ideology, can we gather up the gang and focus on clearing my name?" Notes of anxiety and weariness edged Minx's comment.

Mary grabbed two more cookies from the plate

71

with a smile. "The Scooby gang to the rescue."

Minx fluffed her head. "That's perfect. We already have a Great Dane and one pretty redhead."

"You're not a real redhead," I said.

"You think Daphne was? And we both have a good-looking but kinda dumb guy."

Tiger laughed. "My specialty."

"We have an annoying know-it-all," Minx continued.

Minx and Tiger looked at me.

"Hey," I said, "Velma's not a know-it-all; she's the smart one. Does that mean that Mary is supposed to be Shaggy, the pot-head?"

We turned to look at Mary, whose mouth was full of cookies, and Moo who was snuffling the crumbs off the ground around her. She raised her hand to stop the allegation. "He's not a pot-head," Mary said. "It's a children's show for goodness's sakes. He is just a lovable guy that likes to eat. I think y'all are underestimating his brilliance. Come here, Moo. I'll grab you a Scooby snack."

She got up and reached into the desk drawer where I kept treats for Moo. She gave him one and shoved the rest of the handful into her pocket.

I had to tease Minx a little. "I don't remember Daphne as being such a scrapper. Did I miss the episode where she threw down?"

"Oh geez, do we have to discuss that? I'm having a bad month, okay?"

Mary broke up some of her third cookie and offered it to Minx. "What's going on?"

I had been meaning to ask her about the comment she'd made at the coaches' course many weeks ago. "I was surprised that you're here at all. I thought you said that you weren't going to apply to be an OSA because you didn't want to be in the Middle-of-Nowhere, Wyoming?" I added.

"Things change. Can we focus on who killed Mac right now and save my therapy session for another time?" Minx sulked.

Indy and Mouse were at the door to my office. She was clinging to his side, and he had an arm protectively around one shoulder.

"Hey, guys, can you believe there was a murder, so whack." Indy put a backpack on the ground and leaned up against the doorway.

Mouse scooted in closer to him. "I can't believe this is happening. I wanted to leave right away, but it's snowing so hard out there. But Indy'll protect me, won't you?" She batted her eyelashes up at him and giggled. She didn't look particularly scared, but what did I know?

"Yeah, it's a real shock. What are you guys going to do? You should probably stay out of Brian's way while he investigates."

"Yeah, yeah, yeah, I know." Indy flipped his hair out of his face. "I told Mouse that I could teach her how to play this awesome video game; she would be a great healer. I was hoping you would let her use your computer. I got my laptop from my room."

I wasn't crazy about the idea of them hanging out in my office.

Mouse looked around. "What are you guys going to do?"

Dragging Indy around might be a bit conspicuous when I throttled him for annoying me. "You can use my office. Let me just get everything set for you to use. Tiger, Minx, we'll meet you at the Christmas tree."

I set to logging off my computer with admin privileges and logging back in as a guest so Indy could use the Internet. To break the awkward silence, I explained what I was doing, to which he would reply, "Yeah, yeah, yeah, I know." Each time he said it, my jaw clenched a bit tighter.

I created a throw-away password for him to use and started writing it down. "In order to log use this pass—"

Indy cut me off. "Yeah, yeah, yeah, I know."

I stopped writing midway through the word and took a slow, deep breath. I needed to address this issue, but I needed to do it correctly. I tried to call up my most patient tone. "Indy, please stop saying you know everything. I'm doing you a favor. You can just say okay or thank you."

"Yeah, yeah, yeah, totally, thank you."

I rolled my eyes, but I couldn't complain when he was willing to listen. "You're welcome." I finished writing out the password. Grabbing Moo, I took off his harness and leash then tucked them into the desk. Moo shook his head then all the way down to his tail. His tail snapped back and forth, catching Indy twice on the thigh then once right in his crotch. Indy doubled over with a yip.

"Are you okay?" I asked.

Indy had his eyes squeezed shut, and in a high voice, he said, "Yeah, yeah, yeah, I'm fine."

I tried my best not to chuckle as I headed for the

door. "Please try to be respectful of my office, and if you need anything, please come get me."

Moo bounded into the hallway, dancing and hopping away then back to Mary and me as we walked. He would smash into us then bounce off in a different direction.

Mary pulled a small treat nugget from her pocket. "Do you wanna Scooby snack?"

Moo bounded over and sat in front of her. It was the one trick he knew, and whenever he wanted something, he would sit over and over until he got it. She offered it to him, and he carefully picked it out of her hand then enthusiastically scarfed it down.

"I thought you were going to kill Indy. I could hear your teeth grinding from across the room."

I rolled my eyes. "Please tell me that he isn't an OSA candidate. I might lose my mind if I had to work with him daily."

"I don't think he is. I think he's here because of his dad."

We were slowly walking down the hallway in no real rush. "Who's his dad?"

"Cold," Mary said with a snicker.

"So the annoying apple didn't fall far from the

obnoxious tree."

Mary snorted. When I had met Cold, Indy wasn't around, and he left before Indy returned. I tried to remember if I had missed any clues. He had said that Minx and Kandi had both dated his dad, as had M.C.

As we passed the conference room, I ducked in and signaled for Mary to follow me for a quick private conversation. "Do you know the deal with Minx, Kandi, Mac, and Cold? Some sorta weird love square?"

"No, I don't, but Kandi, Minx, and Cold are all suspects, so we need to find out what happened." She pulled the list from her pocket. Another death, another list from Mary.

"The people on the list were Kandi, Minx, and Cold—like I said. Plus, Orion, M.C., Loggin, and Bucky."

"Who's Bucky?" I had met everyone else on the list, most of them this morning.

"I vaguely know him. He started Bucky Sights; they only make compound sights. You know, the ones with all the pins, like they use in bow hunting?"

"Uh, not really. So where do we start on this investigation? We have done this before, so we should be awesome at it this time." I leaned over to stare at the list.

"I don't know. Last time, I knew everyone, at least vaguely. This time, I have only met half the people in passing. I know Minx, but beyond that…"

I nodded. I had been gung ho to start but felt at an impasse before we even started. "What do you think about Tiger and Minx helping to investigate?"

Mary pulled a sour face then wiped it clean like a blank slate. "I don't know. I like them, but Minx has been moody and snappy since she arrived. Tiger is so smart and dashing, but this is kinda our thing."

"Isn't she always like that?" So far Minx and I had had a rough go at it. She was either fighting with me or teasing me; I found neither particularly fun.

Mary rolled her eyes at me. "No, she's not like this. I don't know why you two don't get along, other than you're too much alike."

I started to object, but Mary held up her hand. "Minx is a smart aleck that has a joke for every situation and isn't afraid to say it like it is. Sound like anyone?"

"My jokes are funny," I muttered under my breath before continuing. "Why don't we talk to Minx about what is going on first, then we can bring cookies to the rest of the suspects. See if anyone volunteers any info and go from there?"

Mary stuffed the list into her pocket. "Better than nothing."

Death at the Summit

CHAPTER SIX

Walking down the hallway to the dining room, where the Christmas tree was set up, I picked up a random dog toy on the floor. I tossed it for Moo, and he bounded ahead to grab it then raced back. The cafeteria was off limits to Moo, but the dining room was separate. It was used as a casual hang-out area for the center, and the tables had been arranged around a large Christmas tree.

The Christmas tree was real, as evidenced by the pile of needles that where vacuumed up a few times a day by the janitorial staff. The tree was covered in an assortment of ornaments from shiny, plastic balls to expensive custom ornaments to handmade paper ornaments made by Mary and me. For the past month, when we weren't working or shooting, we'd been crafting. There were bows, guns, and Great Danes covering the tree.

The center had traded names of those who wanted to exchange gifts, and the wrapped boxes sat under the tree. Mary and I had made little gift bags for the employees together. Until my divorce was final and the assets were broken up, I was living on my meager salary.

The air was filled with the quiet sound of Christmas songs, which had replaced the local station's selection of pop and country music. The scent of cinnamon caught my nose from a basket of pinecones covered in glitter sitting on a small table in the entrance.

Tiger and Minx were sitting near the tree, but Orion and Liam were across the room. I gave Tiger and Minx the just-one-second sign then went over to say hi to Orion and Liam.

"Hey, how are you guys?"

Orion chuckled. "Oh great. Who doesn't want to be a suspect in a murder?"

"Oh, it's not so bad. Don't tell Brian, but Mary and I will figure it out." I gave Orion a friendly pat on the shoulder then pulled out a chair to sit in.

"I forget that you have been through this before." Orion sat back in his chair.

Liam looked at me and stood abruptly. "I'm going to check on Mom."

As he walked away abruptly, I asked Orion, "Is he okay? He has seemed... off all day."

Orion stared after Liam with a distracted look on his face. "He's fine. He's probably just worried about the murder." He continued to stare after Liam before shaking his head and turning back to me. He flashed me a brilliant smile, and I was struck by how handsome he was. Then a wash of unease came over me. I cast my eyes back to Liam then squirmed in my seat as I tamped down any thoughts about Orion's looks.

Mary sat down in Liam's vacant chair. "He seems about the same as always to me."

Maybe Mary was right, though something felt different to me. "Is there anything I can do for you? We can unlock the weight room if you want to burn off some energy."

Orion looked down at his outfit. "I wish I could. What I really want to do is work, but not much chance at that. Practically everyone is back at the hotel."

I waved my hand at Tiger, and when he saw me, I signaled him to come over. "I might be able to help you. Tiger was telling us earlier that your speech this morning inspired him."

Tiger joined us and shook Orion's hand.

"Tiger, you should tell Orion your idea about a women-only class at the center."

Mary and I excused ourselves as Tiger started explaining his idea to Orion. We went over to Minx, who was sitting in a chair with her head in her hands.

Mary pulled up a chair next to her and patted her on the back. "What's going on?"

Minx shook her head, and through her hands, she mumbled, "I don't want to be here anymore."

My heart broke for her a little bit. "How about we get you some hot cider?"

She nodded. I called for Moo, who was on the far side of the room, trying to dig a potato chip from under some furniture.

Grabbing Minx's elbow, I led her into the cafeteria. It was empty, which was good because Moo was not allowed in there. He took it upon himself to check the entire floor for crumbs, a task that could have taken him all day. The workers must have been released earlier because of all the snow warnings. I made up several cups of cider and brought them over to a table where Mary was sitting next to Minx.

I took a small sip of the cider and decided it was still too hot. I cupped my hands around the warmth. "What's going on, Minx?" She started to protest, and I held up a hand. "I know you don't want to discuss it, but you seem to know all the suspects better than us. You dated Mac and Cold."

She choked on her cider. "I did *not* date Mac. That's a lie. Who said that? If it was Kandi, I'll kill her."

"It wasn't Kandi. I haven't even met her. Do you want to tell us what did happen?"

Minx flopped back in her seat. "Fine. This was a long time ago. I met Cold at the Vegas tournament."

"What Vegas tournament?" This was the second time that I had heard about it today.

Mary swirled her cider with a cinnamon stick. "Every year, around Valentine's Day, there's a three-day tournament in Las Vegas. Everyone just calls it 'the Vegas tournament.' I think it's the biggest in the world. It definitely has the biggest payout in America. People come from all over the world, and in America, anyone who's anyone attends. Normally, the 3D archers stick to their tournaments shooting foam animals, and the field archers do their field tournaments while we do ours. There's some crossover between the types, mostly

85

between 3D and field archers and a tiny bit between field and the target archery we do. But everyone goes to Vegas. It's in a casino off the Strip. Plus, all the companies attend, so the average person can see the new equipment lines and pick up supplies directly from the suppliers. We'll have to go in February."

Minx seemed eager to get back to her story. "So I met Cold there one year, and we kinda flirted all year online or in text messages. Saw each other once or twice. He wasn't doing his video work then; he was competing in 3D. The next year at the tournament, he swept me off my feet. Told me how great I was and took me on this super-fancy date in the nicest restaurant."

"So you *did* date Cold?" He seemed like such a jerk.

She waved a hand at me. "He used to be much cuter, but really it was only that one official date. The next day, we were hanging out in the afternoon at the casino, and we ran into Kandi. That was it. When Cold and Kandi made eye contact, he stopped talking mid-sentence and said he would be right back. I guess they hooked back up that very night. Someone said they had dated years before."

"How long ago was this?"

She shrugged. "I don't know. Six years, eight years, something like that."

It had to have been a bummer and been embarrassing but if Minx was holding a grudge over that, it was petty. "So you hate Kandi 'cause she stole your boyfriend?"

"That was just the first of many things: snide remarks here or making the point to correct me in public. Her best friend competed against me, and we had a few dustups. And she didn't date Cold for long. She turned around and married Mac like a year or two later."

"Why does she hate you?"

"That wasn't my fault!"

"Jinkies! What happened?"

"A couple years ago, MacSights was considering an expansion into recurve sights. Mac and I started talking about recurve sights over the Internet and he suggested I come out, take a tour of the factory, give my input, *et cetera*."

Maybe I was just older and wiser but that smelled like trouble. "Oh, Minx."

"I know. Now, it's totally obvious. I mean he paid for my plane ticket and offered to let me stay at his house. I insisted on a hotel because I didn't want to be around Kandi. But guess what?"

"Kandi wasn't there?"

She played with her fingers. "Nope, she was out of town, visiting her mom. He gives me a tour. Then we go into his office, and he's telling me that I was so talented and pretty that I could be the new face of MacSights. Then he tries to kiss me, and Kandi comes in."

Mary shook her head. "That's awful."

"I swear, I didn't encourage him at all. I was flattered by the attention, but I never thought it was about anything other than my archery ability and great ideas, but Kandi starts screaming about me trying to seduce her husband. I just grabbed my purse and got out of there. MacSights ended up not making recurve sights."

Mary nodded. "I heard they didn't have the money to invest in a new line."

"No, that couldn't be. They were making money hand over fist. They started that Kandi-covered line right afterward."

Mary shrugged and took another sip from her cider.

"I haven't seen either of them in years."

"Until today." I took a sip from my cider, too. The spicy warmth was comforting and familiar.

"We were done with our task and were coming to join you guys when I ran into Kandi, literally. I had no idea they would be here. She said something about trying to steal what's hers, then I said something about looking for new milk when the cow is old. Then next thing I know, she shoved me, and I slapped her. It felt amazing for a split second, then I was so embarrassed. Did you guys see it?"

"Yes, we all did. In fact, Cold filmed it."

Minx straightened in her seat. "He what! That will ruin me. We have to get it."

Mary patted her shoulder. "Don't worry; Di took care of it."

I slapped my pocket. "I got the memory card right here. You're fine. Why didn't you just ignore her when she said something?"

Minx scrubbed her face and blew out a sigh. "It's been a bad few months. I've been living with my parents since college to save money so I can train. The plan was that after I returned from the Summer Games, I would move out with two of my sisters and we would live on our own. Tons of my friends are married, many have kids, but at the very least, they are not living with their parents. My sisters have been dragging their feet on moving out, and in the past month, both have gotten engaged. They're going to live at home until the weddings. I'm thrilled for them but it has me feeling… left behind."

I got up, snatched a plate of cookies off the counter, and brought them over to share. "Depressed?"

"I don't know. It isn't just that. I have been training to make the Summer Games for years and years. I thought it would complete me. And it happened and was amazing, but I'm still the same person. Nothing really changed. I don't feel any different. Now I don't feel like doing anything, even things I used to like. I'm short-tempered and snapping at everyone. I just want to be left alone. That's why I decided to apply to be an On-Site Athlete here. I need a new chapter in my life. A big change. Something."

My divorce had been a rough time for me, and I still wasn't fully over it, but I was much better than I had been.

"That sounds like what I went through after my divorce. It got worse and worse until at one point, I curled up on the couch in a blanket and barely moved for weeks. The Summer Games were on TV. I watched all of it, including the archers shoot. I must have watched you shoot, though I don't remember. I couldn't imagine ever being happy again and didn't have a clue what to do next. Then I talked to Jess, and she mentioned the job opening, and suddenly, I was driving to Wyoming. Now I have this new life and couldn't be happier. You will figure out where you should be."

Minx seemed a bit encouraged. A small smile caught the corner of her mouth.

"Do you know M.C. at all?"

She shook her head. "Not really beyond a conversation here and there. I'm so embarrassed because clearly, he knew why his dad invited me out there, and he thought I was up for it. M.C. likes nice things like vacations, cars, and clothing and he's the marketing director for MacSights. That's about all I know. But he doesn't matter—Kandi killed Mac. She has been fooling around for years from what I've heard, and she wants all that money."

"Mac had a lot of money?"

"Totally, they're the biggest sight company in the industry."

"Minx, we've been looking for you."

We all turned to see that Jess was at the door of the cafeteria with Brian. "Brian needs to talk to you."

Minx went a little pale, and her eyes were wide. Mary reached over and gave her a hug. "It'll be okay. Brian's nice."

CHAPTER SEVEN

Minx left with Brian, and Jess took her seat. Her face was blank, but her hands picked up a napkin and preceded to carefully accordion fold it one way then the other. She would flatten it out then do it again.

After the fifth time, I interjected. "You feeling okay?"

"Fine. Fine. I'm fine." She didn't look up but shifted into folding the napkin in half over and over until it was too thick to fold again. She unfolded it, smoothed it out, turned it ninety degrees and started again.

"Do you want some cider?" I asked. Perhaps a warm drink would perk her up. "Hot chocolate?"

She looked at me with wide, round eyes as she started folding the napkin diagonally. "Hot chocolate?

Do we have any mini marshmallows?"

I nodded and made the most decadent hot chocolate I could: whole milk, a handful of mini marshmallows, and the perfect temperature. The warm, rich smell made my mouth water. I handed it to Jess, and she took a deep breath. Her shoulders relaxed, and after a sip, she closed her eyes. When she opened them, the tightness was gone and so was her death grip on the napkin. "That's nice. Are there any more cookies?"

We turned to Mary, who was just chewing the last of the cookies from the plate. She got up with the plate. "I'm sure there's more in the kitchen."

Jess turned back to me. "I'm not sure if I can handle the stress of this job. What if there's a murder every time I host an event?"

I smiled at her. "Then we'll get a lot of experience solving crimes."

"This isn't a joke, Di."

"I'm not joking. It'll be okay. Who do you think killed Mac? The sooner we figure it out, the sooner you can relax."

Jess rolled her eyes at me. "It could be anyone; he was awful. After that fight this morning, everyone got pulled out to have a firm talking-to about appropriate

Westmound behavior. I thought he was going to hit Kandi. I wouldn't be surprised if he has before. Orion stepped in. Mac kept calling him 'boy.' I can't imagine that Westmound would have kept him much longer."

Mary came back with three undecorated cookies in the shape of angels. "I guess they ran out of time to finish all the cookies. Mac sounds awful. His son, M.C., said he was a bigot. Is that attitude common?"

Jess sat back and was quiet before she answered. "Yes and no. I think that at least nine out of ten people in the industry are awesome and aren't concerned about gender or ethnicity. They care about our industry and want to do what's best. A customer is a customer. But if one person out of ten dismisses you or your ideas because you are female or a minority, then it's a big problem. They don't have to say why they are against you; they can just say, 'Oh, I don't think that's a good idea.' For instance, there've been a few times I have proposed ideas, and they were shot down as financially unviable or wouldn't work. But then within a year, a guy suggested it, and everyone went on and on about what a great innovative idea it was. Now, maybe that was a coincidence, but when it keeps happening, you have to wonder. Plus there are a couple people like Mac that will flat out say that minorities and women aren't an important part of our industry."

"Dude, that sucks." I had spent almost a decade in the technology field fighting the idea that women and technology didn't mix. It never had occurred to me that I might have to deal with the same issues here.

"Like I said, most people and companies are awesome. Westmound is one of the best. Plus, Mac is gone, so one less person to worry about. Maybe that opinion will go extinct like the dinosaurs."

"Like a racisaurus." Mary snorted.

We groaned but couldn't keep from smiling.

Jess finished off her cocoa. "Thanks for cheering me up. I'm going to see if I can help out with anything. You two stay out of trouble or at least pretend." Jess turned to look at Moo on the floor next to the table. He had managed to pull the sweat shirt up over his head but not completely off. He flipped back and forth, his head obscured behind the stretchy red fabric covered with tiny glitter snowflakes. "You, too, Moo."

CHAPTER EIGHT

"We should take Moo outside." I removed the sweatshirt from Moo's head then took our cups into the kitchen and loaded them into the dishwasher.

We left the cafeteria with Moo leading the way. Instead of heading into the hallway, he veered the other way, back into the dining room. Spread throughout the room were the various suspects whom Brian had held back, minus Minx. Moo ran up to Loggin, and we followed.

"Is this your dog?" Loggin looked between Mary and me as we approached.

"He belongs to Liam, but he spends his days with me." I scratched Moo's rump.

"Cool, he's an awesome dog. Where's the other gal?"

"Who?" There were a lot of gals around. I had a

suspicion whom he meant.

"Pretty, red hair. She yelled at me earlier. What's her name? Does she work here? Is she an archer?" He kept a casual tone.

I chuckled. "Her name is Minx. She doesn't work here, and she is a very good archer."

"Really? What kind?"

I looked at Mary, who was smiling at his obvious questions. "She shoots target recurve and competed in the Summer Games this last summer."

"Wow. I want to apologize to her. Do you think you could…?"

"I'll see if I can help you out. Did you get your really serious problem solved?" He had been pretty upset earlier.

"I think Orion will help me out. He needs to finish talking to that guy over there, then he's going to try to introduce me to Elizabeth and Liam Andersson."

I looked at where Tiger and Orion were still talking, then turned back to Loggin. "Good luck."

***

Stepping outside, I was blown away how by different everything looked. The world was white; the sky, the ground, and even the horizon had disappeared.

The housing units were hidden, and after I'd stepped a few dozen feet into the parking lot, the center vanished behind me. Moo took off at a dead run and disappeared.

I grabbed Mary's arm while calling to Moo. "Moo! This is crazy. Is there any way to drive in this?"

"I don't think so. I think everyone is stuck until it stops and the snowplows get out here."

It was still early afternoon, but it felt like it was twilight. Moo zoomed out of the snow. His front legs rose high over the piling snow. He leaped up then landed deeply, sending out sprays of snow, as he approached. His back legs splayed wildly as they landed. He sped toward us and hit the space between Mary and me. The force of the blow was not as severe as the one was yesterday since it was split between us. I braced myself but still hit the ground hard. In a repeat of yesterday, I lay there for a second, catching my breath.

"You okay?" I called out to Mary, who had also gone flying.

"Geez, Moo, what was that about?" Mary was already getting up and wiping off the snow.

"Sorry, I should've warned you. Liam said that Moo has a problem with playing too rough in the snow."

"Thanks a lot. That would have been super-useful information to have had five minutes ago."

Moo reappeared from the whiteness and skidded to a stop in front of us. His tongue hung out, and he was breathing heavily, with a big doggy grin on his face. He started sniffing around for a spot to do his business.

"What do you think about what Minx said?"

Mary kicked at the snow. "Poor gal, I know just what she is feeling. After my mom got so sick, I felt the same way. But once I moved here, I started to feel better. Starting to shoot again has helped a lot, too."

I nodded. I hadn't grabbed gloves, and the cool air bit into my hands. I shoved them into my pocket only to run up against the small, hard memory chip. "We should watch the video of the fight. Think there will be anything important?"

Mary shrugged. "You never know." She wrapped her arms around her middle. "Let's get back inside."

I looked out at the snow then back at the center. We were trapped here with a dead body. "Do you think they'll replace the carpeting?"

Mary turned to me blankly. "What?"

"All that blood. Mac's dead body's in that room and we're stuck at the center. It's kinda freaking me out."

We stood and stared at the center. Mary gave a little shiver. "I wasn't freaked out before, but now I am. Thanks a lot."

"What can I say? Misery loves company."

Moo finished his business and kicked snow over the area with stiff, awkward legs. He ran back to the door. I looked over the snow that was still falling heavily and headed toward the door, stumbling over a parking block obscured by the snow. "Wow, I can't believe how much snow there is."

Mary held open the door. "Welcome to Wyoming."

We chuckled and dusted ourselves off before going into the main hallway with Moo. Noises bounced down the hallways from the various people trapped in the center, even though no one was in sight. I wondered where Brian was interviewing people. Where was Liam, who seemed to appear and disappear randomly? My office was a short distance down the hallway, but long before we reached the office, we could hear Indy's excited voice.

"Icebolt, Icebolt, use your cool down. Ice Burst! You got him. Great job."

I stepped into the office, and Indy leaped back

from Mouse. She was staring intently at the laptop screen with her face all scrunched up in concentration.

Indy's face turned red for a second, then he seemed to pull himself together. "Mouse is an awesome caster. She's a natural at DPS. I got her started on my computer, but as soon as the game downloads on your computer, we're going to run some dungeons."

"Uh…" That was a lot of words that made no sense. "I need the office for a bit. Can you both clear out for about ten minutes?"

"Do we have to? The game only needs like five more minutes."

"Perfect, then when we are done, your game will be downloaded, and you can play."

"Yeah, yeah, yeah, okay. Come on, Mouse, I can introduce you to my dad." He offered her his hand, and tentatively, she grabbed it. They left the room hand in hand.

After they were gone, I raised an eyebrow at Mary. "The holding-hands thing is new."

"At least someone is having a good day." She pulled out the chair that Indy had been sitting in and sat.

I slid the memory card into a reader and waited for the computer to register it. Opening up the folders, I saw two video clips; one from today and one from the previous month. After I clicked on the clip from today, the video popped up on the screen.

The footage popped around on the screen as Cold got the camera settled on the action. Minx was on the screen, facing off with Kandi. The audio wasn't loud enough to hear what they were saying, but the body language made up for it. Kandi shoved Minx hard. Even knowing what was coming, I was shocked when Minx slapped Kandi.

When Minx's hand hit Kandi's cheek and she disappeared from frame, I couldn't help when a snort of laughter escaped. I rewound and watched again, laughing even harder. Then I rewound and added commentary. "You have something on your face." *Slap!* "Let me introduce you to my little friend." *Slap!* "Kandi-covered slap." *Slap!* I was laughing so hard, I could barely talk.

Mary tried to suppress a giggle. "You are enjoying this a bit too much."

I tried to stop laughing. "Sorry, you're right. See anything new?"

She pointed to the background on the screen, where Mac was arguing with a thin man. "That's Bucky.

He's on the list."

"Oh, I saw him fighting with Mac when the fight first occurred. He's one of the suspects? Interesting."

I rewound until I found the point where Mac and Bucky started interacting. Mac said something with a smug smile. Bucky's face was tense and angry. They went back for forth until the fight was broken up. The whole time, Mac smirked while Bucky's face got redder and angrier.

"We need to see if we can get Bucky to tell us what they fought about." I closed the video player and clicked the other video on the card. The camera appeared to be sitting on a desk or table and was pointed at a bed in an otherwise-empty room. A man's voice was talking, and then he looked into the camera. It was Cold, and he was on the phone.

"Don't ever put that in writing again. No e-mail, no texts, nothing."

He walked around the room as he listened to the phone.

"Yeah, I can get it. Just remember, if this gets into food, it would kill someone, and if it was spicy or flavorful, they would never taste it. So I am saying not to do that. You're such an idiot, I swear. Okay. Bye."

A few seconds later, the video ended.

"What was that about?" Mary asked.

I shook my head and we watched the short clip three more times. We leaned in close to the screen, straining to hear more details, but nothing more revealed itself.

A chill crept over me. "Do you want to watch again?" Mary shook her head, and I popped the memory card out and put it on my desk. "That was ominous. Do you think he was getting poison for someone? Or convincing someone not to poison someone? Why did he film that? Is this connected to Mac's murder or something different?" I had so many questions that were unanswerable.

"I don't know, but this doesn't add up. Could Mac could have been poisoned?"

I dropped the sweat shirt I had removed from Moo under the desk then opened his drawer to pull out a different Christmas vest. Moo shoved his head between us and nuzzled the drawer, which also held treats. I grabbed the container of treats and gave him one. Then I wrestled the vest onto him. It was green-and-red plaid with a Christmas tree on his back. "I don't think so. Is there a poison that would make you bleed a bunch? We need to give this to Brian right away."

Moo bumped the container hard with his nose, and treats spilled over the desk. He was right on top of them, but before I could do more than yell out his name, Moo had picked the desk clean of every treat.

Mary leaped from her chair. "No, no, no, Moo!"

"What's wrong?"

"The memory card is gone."

I grabbed Moo and lifted his right jowl then the left one then pried his mouth open. Nothing was inside but massive teeth and his tongue. "Maybe he just knocked it on the floor." I crawled onto the floor to check.

Mary flopped into the chair. "No, I saw it disappear into this mouth. What do we tell Brian?"

"Nothing, we say nothing. If anyone asks, we flushed it down the toilet hours ago. That video was too weird. Don't tell anyone—that includes Minx and Tiger."

"Why not just tell the truth that Moo ate the card?"

"Do you think anyone would believe the dog ate the evidence? That sounds an awful lot like 'the dog ate my homework.' Let's just say that right after he gave me the card, I flushed it without looking at it."

Mary nodded. "Okay, that works. Something about

that video was really off."

Chills crept up my arms, and I rubbed them, hoping to knock the feeling away.

CHAPTER NINE

Walking down the hall, I kept an eye on Moo, watching him for choking or intestinal discomfort. I had looked around on the web, and Great Danes had been known to have eaten much larger things with no harm, but that didn't mean I felt good about it.

Mary sidled up to me, whispering so her voice wouldn't carry, list of suspects in hand. "Wanna talk to Bucky next? Maybe we can see what he and Mac were fighting about."

"I'm gonna try a bluff. Just go along with me."

Mary rolled her eyes at me. "I think I know how to investigate a murder. Geez, this isn't my first time."

"Two murders, and now we're experts, eh?" I chucked.

Heading toward the dining area, we spotted Bucky alone. Sneaking Moo in, we headed over to Bucky.

"Hi, Bucky, right?" I extended my hand. "I'm Di, and this is Mary. We work here at the Westmound Center. Is there anything I can get you?"

He stood to shake my hand then introduced himself to Mary before sitting back down and shaking his head.

"Do you mind if we sit? We heard about the fight you had with Mac and thought you might want to…" I purposely trailed off then sat quietly, looking at him. I was hoping that he would feel compelled to defend himself.

Bucky's mouth pursed up, his cheeks puffed out, then he blew out a hard breath. "You have to understand, I am thrilled to work for Westmound. Elizabeth and the whole company have been great. My issue is not with them."

Mary and I both nodded while I said, "Of course, understandable," in what I hoped was a great impression of understanding.

He looked between Mary and me as we nodded, then he continued. "That being said, I will never forgive Mac for what he did. That is not what this industry is about. Cheating, deception, and cutthroat practices have no place here. We are about honesty, family, and community."

I nodded while frantically trying to figure out how to get him to explain without breaking our bluff. "Do you want to tell us, in your words, what happened?"

His face was red, and the muscles in his jaw flexed. He stared intently at the table until, in a rush, he started talking. "Remember when the bowhunter division rules were changed suddenly eight years ago?"

I didn't know what the bowhunter division meant beyond the fact that in tournaments, a "division" meant a class in competition that was defined by what equipment was used in the tournament. I certainly didn't know about rule changes.

Mary took over. "Yes, though the details are a bit fuzzy right now."

He swung around to her, raking a hand through his hair, then undid the top button on his shirt, which had been straining again his throat. "Most of my sales were from archers competing in the bowhunter division. We had a brand-new line coming out that met the current rules at great expense to the company. Then suddenly, two months before the competition season, the rules committee announced a change to rules regarding sights in the bowhunter division. Suddenly, my entire line of products was not allowed. But guess what company had just launched several new lines of sights that just happened to meet the new rules?"

"MacSights," Mary and I said in unison.

"Yep, you got it. It was too close to the season to get out any new products, and our sales essentially went to zero overnight. There was no way to recover. Rather than firing my employees, I sold to Westmound. I don't regret that choice, but I regret having to make the choice at all. Mac deserved all that he got and more. If life was fair, he would have been forced to sell his company to Westmound, but instead, he got to decide when and how to sell his company."

"So you think he had some hand in changing the rules?" I needed to make sure I understood rather than just assuming.

He slammed his palm down hard on the table, making both Mary and me jump. "Of course! Don't be naïve. He bribed or blackmailed them. I heard the three members of the committee went hunting with Mac for years. I think a couple of the members resigned shortly afterward. I wasn't the only company that was upset about the rule changes but I was affected the most. We rallied and protested. The rule was eventually modified, but by then, all the archers had bought new equipment from MacSights, and I was in the hole so far that I could never crawl out."

Mary shook her head. "That's not right."

"No, it's *not* right. People shouldn't be able to win when they are cheaters. And I told him as much today. He just laughed at me. It took everything in me not to punch him." His voice was rising with each sentence. Suddenly, he leaned forward, imploring us. "You have to convince Elizabeth to clean house at MacSights. The whole family is corrupt. I know that M.C. was part of that rules situation. He is a cheat through and through. And Kandi is trouble, cold and calculating. I'm surprised she didn't knife Mac in his sleep. She only married him for the money. They're going to ruin Westmound if they stay. Poison, both of them." He was heaving huge breaths.

Moo whined next to me and huddled in close. I wrapped an arm around Moo's frame and rubbed his side. Bucky's intensity was unsettling. "I'll mention it to Liam."

Bucky sat back in his seat, relaxed. His face was no longer red, and he casually crossed a leg onto the opposite knee. "Thank you. Liam's a good guy. I can't say how grateful I am that Mac is dead. I think I will throw a party when I get home." He cupped his hands around a cup of coffee and smiled.

I stood up. "That sounds nice." No, it didn't. It sounded insane. "If you need anything, let us know."

Mary mirrored my actions, and we practically ran out of the cafeteria and smacked right into M.C.

He snorted. "What are you gals running from?" He looked over our shoulders. "Oh, Bucky, paranoid old goat. He's such a weirdo. Business is business, but he's a stick in the mud. I'm bored. Will you entertain me for a bit?" He had a broad smile and friendly nature.

"Sure, we have a few minutes." And a few questions. After we followed him back into the dining room, he pulled out chairs for Mary and me. On the far side of the room, Loggin gave us a quick glance before he looked away.

I remembered Mac was M.C.'s father. "How are you holding up, M.C.?"

He waved a hand in the air. "I think I'm in shock but also not surprised. Dad was an aggressive man. You live by the sword; you die by the sword. That's how life is meant to be. Too many pansies around, unwilling and unable to do what needs to be done for success. Those that were weak resented Dad. Like Bucky—every time we ran into him he was like, 'Wah wah you ruined my life. Boo hoo!' What a sap."

I had thought the conversation with Bucky was awkward, but this was taking it to a new level. Mary shifted in her seat next to me then poked me in the side.

"You think he killed your dad?"

"Could be. Or Kandi. Or Cold. Or Loggin. Or Orion. Or Minx. Or heck, maybe one of you. The list is endless." He leaned back in his chair and kicked his feet on the table to reveal turquoise cowboy boots.

"But not you?" The question popped out. I held my breath—I had just accused M.C. of killing his father. How heartless was I?

He took it all in stride. "Why would I kill my father? I loved him and had nothing to gain. Dad was no idiot. Kandi's hot, but she's not trustworthy. He gave me my inheritance before the wedding. The company was doing well, and we both got enough from our salary. You're admiring my boots, aren't you?"

The boots were distracting. They weren't exactly good looking, but they were hard to look away from.

"I got them in Spain last year. They were handcrafted by a man that had the secrets of leatherworking passed down to him through five generations. The leather is artisan tanned then formed with hand tools. The whole process took months, and the final step was to form them specifically to my feet. I shouldn't tell you how much they cost, but if you promise not to tell, they were fourteen thousand dollars. I am thinking of getting a second set."

I was at a loss for words. I didn't know boots could cost that much and couldn't imagine ever having enough money to justify that kind of price tag. "Wow. That is...... wow."

"Nice, huh? Not everyone can appreciate the finer things in life, but when you have good taste, you see things others don't." He admired his boots some more.

Mary seemed mesmerized by the boots. I saw her mouth, "Fourteen thousand," a few times then tentatively reach out to pet one.

M.C. smiled widely. "Go on, touch one. They feel like butter, don't they?"

She stroked the toe of the boot a few times then ran a finger over the embroidery along the side. "Wow."

Taking her hand back, she looked at him. I elbowed her in the side. She shook her head and pulled herself out of her trance.

"Nice boots," I said. "Uh, what does M.C. stand for? I have always wondered."

"I'm named after my dad. He's MacIntosh Davis, and I'm MacIntosh Davis II. When I was born, people started calling him Big Mac and me Little Mac. Obviously. I didn't want to go by Little Mac forever so I switched to M.C. around fifteen and people dropped the 'Big' from his nickname."

"Do you know why someone would kill your dad?" I tried to bring the conversation back around.

"He made some nasty remarks to Orion. I told you about Bucky. I'm pretty sure Kandi was fooling around. Minx was still mad about that time she tried to seduce Dad and Kandi busted her. Loggin was pissed that his sponsorship deal fell through and kept threatening us. Who knows? People are jealous of success, and Dad was definitely successful." He looked over our shoulder, sat up, and stomped his boots onto the floor. "Looks like it's my turn to talk to the police."

Brian stood at the entrance to the dining area. Brian's eyes landed on us, and he headed our way. "Can I speak with you, sir?"

"Sure thing, officer." M.C. gave us a wink, stood, and started to leave with Brian.

I burst out of my seat. "Brian, wait, can I talk to you for a second? Privately."

"Sure. Wait here, M.C."

M.C. leaned against a wall while Brian and I went into the hallway.

"Uh, how did Mac die? Stabbing? Bludgeoning? Shooting? Poisoning?"

Brian shook his head through my questions, but when I got to poisoning, he snorted. "Definitely not poisoning. I told you I'm not telling you how he died. You didn't find something, did you?"

"No, sir, I have nothing to share with you."

He raised an eyebrow. "I'm suspicious when you call me 'sir.'"

"I have nothing to share with you, you big doofus."

He chuckled and shook his head. "That's better. Now if you have nothing to share, then let me get back to work."

I went back to sit with Mary, only to spot Minx hesitating in the doorway. At the far side of the room, Loggin watched her from the edge of his seat.

I scooted my chair around so my back was to him, and patted the seat next to me. Minx came over and sat down.

"How was it?"

Minx sighed dramatically and flopped her head down onto the table.

Mary leaned over to pat her back for the millionth time today. "That good, eh?"

Minx rolled her head to the side so that her cheek was resting on the table. "If I wasn't feeling crappy before, then let me tell you, I feel awful now. Explaining the whole story to Brian was beyond embarrassing. I really need to get a handle on my life."

Her voice had a bit more strength to it. Instead of being hollow and wistful, she sounded a bit disgusted.

"Minx, can we speak with you?"

We whipped around to see Elizabeth with Jess behind her. Jess was nervously spinning her phone in her hand.

Minx went a little white. "Yes, ma'am, of course." She stood up, knocking her chair over backward in her haste. Elizabeth's face was impossible to read as they quietly left the room.

"Do you think they are going to tell her that she isn't going to be an OSA?" Mary asked.

I sucked air through my teeth. "Ouch, if that's the case, I think Minx might win the award for the worst day ever. Well, I mean, after Mac."

I checked around the room. Loggin was no longer watching us and was instead intent on his phone.

I scooted over next to Mary. "Get out the list, Shaggy."

She pulled the list out of her pocket with a giggle and smoothed it on the table. Moo shoved his head into the list and gave it a good lick before Mary could move it out of his reach. "I assume that we have already eliminated Orion and Minx, right?"

"Sure, my advanced detective gut tells me that they aren't killers. But M.C. and Bucky— they are still on the list. I think either of them could have done it."

"Definitely. I heard that Bucky is a nice guy, but he was so angry, and M.C. was weird."

"He was pretty casual about the fact that his dad was murdered just a few hours ago. Could he be in shock or something?"

Mar pursed her lips and looked up at the ceiling for a bit before replying, "Maybe. We need to still talk to Loggin."

I followed her gaze across the room to Loggin. He had made a bad first impression this morning. We would need to see what his deal was.

"I need that memory card back." A beefy male hand gripped my upper arm hard.

I let out a yip and reared around to see who it was. Cold's fingers dug into my arm hard, pinching my skin.

"Ouch! Don't touch me like that!" My voice came out angry and aggressive, but inside, I was startled and scared. Moo leaped to his feet and moved close. He let out a growl.

Cold leaned in and hissed in my ear, "Give it to me."

"Di, what's going on here?" Loggin called out as he started to cross the room.

Cold dropped my arm. I rubbed the spot while the two men faced each other. Moo shoved his nose into my face, sniffing me all over while I petted him and spoke softly to him. "It's okay; everything's fine." He pushed his body up against me, pinning me in my chair while placing himself between me and the men.

Cold chuckled while replying, "Hey, no problems, Loggin. I just realized that the memory card I gave them this morning had footage from a friend's wedding. I need it back right now."

Mary's mouth had been hanging open, and she shut it with a snap. "It's gone."

He swung back to us with narrowed eyes. "What do you mean? Where is it?"

I swallowed hard. "I flushed it. I knew that even if we deleted the fight off the card, that it was recoverable, so I had to destroy it. The easiest way was to flush it." Or feed it to a big dog. The hair on Moo's back was sticking straight up. I grabbed his collar as he pushed forward, growling, his teeth bared.

"So it's gone? Like *gone* gone, never coming back?" He said it slowly, considering each word.

"Yes, very gone."

He cast his eyes and seemed to think for a bit before nodding thoughtfully. "That'll work."

"What going on? Is there a party and no one invited me?" Orion called out as he, Tiger, and Liam entered the cafeteria.

Cold grabbed Orion's hand, the palms slapping together loudly, the tendons in their hands and wrists straining visibly in the grip. "No one could have a party without you."

Liam came to my other side and leaned over. "Everything okay?"

I nodded and rubbed my arm. Would I have a bruise there? "We're good now. But it was weird for a while. I'll tell you later."

"It's nice here and all, but seriously, how long are we stuck?" Cold had a huge smile slapped on his face. Gone was any hint of the anger.

Orion sucked air through his teeth and shook his head. "Sorry, man, but we're snowed in. The police can't even make it here until the plows can clear the roads. The snow is supposed to stop this evening, and they have us high up on the priority list."

I knew that no one was supposed to leave, but realizing that no one *could* leave was a bit different, especially after the tense interaction with Cold. I stood up and put more space between us. Mary followed suit. Tiger moved in next to us.

"Loggin, we're ready to meet with you, if you are interested," Orion suggested.

"Absolutely."

Orion gave another look around the group. "Before we go, does anyone need anything else?"

I jerked my head toward the hallway. We started to move off, but Cold had one more question.

"Where's the lost and found? I lost my cell phone earlier."

Mary stopped dead. I crashed into her back, then

Moo bounced into the back of me. With wide eyes, she turned back to Cold. "Camo phone cover? Had initials on the back?"

"Yeah, CHF for Cold Hard Facts, my archery show. Did you find it?"

"Someone turned it in. It's on the center table in the long range. We can go get it." I pushed Mary gently from behind. If that was Cold's phone, then what about the picture on the phone?

"No, I'll go with you to get it. I'd hate for you to accidentally flush it." He moved to follow us.

CHAPTER TEN

"I can't believe that's Cold's phone," I burst out the second I closed the conference room door behind Tiger and Mary. We had taken Cold to the center's table, where he had just identified the missing phone as his. I had made a bee line to a private place where I could discuss the importance of this information.

"I know. Unbelievable." She threw her hands into the air.

"What's the big deal about the phone?" Tiger grabbed a chair and spun it around backward to straddle it.

"Don't tell Cold, but when Mary found the phone, we opened it. There was a picture of…" Suddenly, I felt a bit uncomfortable, but there was no way to explain other than to just say it. "A man's hand on a woman's breast. The woman had a pink-and-white tattoo of a lollypop."

"Kandi," Tiger said.

"So you noticed that tattoo, eh?" I smirked at him.

"Hey, it's a foot tall on the advertisement, plus she pointed it out to me. She said she got it a few weeks ago."

"No way!" I looked at Mary. "That means the photo had to be taken recently. Did you see the way she followed him around? He probably killed Mac, or maybe they did it together."

Mary nodded. "He is such a douche canoe."

I nodded. "My gut says he's dangerous. I don't want to be alone with him, like ever. I don't know if we should talk to him."

Tiger hitched his chin up in the air. "I'm not scared of him."

"It's not a matter of being scared" —I thought about the look in his eyes when he grabbed my arm— "not *only* a matter of being scared. Someone killed Mac, violently. We should be cautious. Plus, Cold doesn't like Mary or me at all. He won't say anything to us."

"If only you had a guy Cold liked to investigate him. That would be super awesome." Moo went to Tiger's side, and Tiger reached over to scratch behind his ears. "You want a Scooby snack, buddy? Moo's Scooby and I'm supposed to be Fred, the leader of the investigation, the handsome guy in charge." Tiger leaned back and balanced on two legs of the chair.

I felt a rush of irritation. "Fred's not in charge. Velma's in charge. I'm the clever one. I mean, Velma's the clever one."

"Fred's the man."

I opened my mouth to protest, then I saw the smirk on his face. "Oh, real funny. So, *man*, you want to talk to Cold? What do you plan on saying?"

He leaned forward and winked. "You're the brains of this operation. You tell me."

He was a flatterer, and it was working. I grabbed a chair and an errant pen. Motioning to Mary to join us, I handed her the pen. "Let's go over what we have so far. We know that Kandi and Cold have something going on."

Mary pulled the list out of her pocket and uncapped the pen, poised to take notes.

Tiger waggled his eyebrows at us. "I'll tell you what they have going on. They're—"

I cut Tiger off. "Having an affair."

He laughed. "That's a polite way of saying it. Is that

all you've figured out?"

"No, we talked to M.C. He says that he won't receive any inheritance from Mac's death. He got it already and lives off his salary. But he had a lot to say about everyone else. Oh, and he pays way too much for boots."

Mary had been staring at Tiger with a goofy smile on her face. When I mentioned the shoes though, she perked up. "Who spends that much on shoes? Even though that was the softest leather I have ever felt and the color was beautiful." She shook herself. "Who can afford that?"

I shrugged. "I guess he gets a nice salary from MacSights. I wonder if that will change now that they are owned by Westmound?"

Mary pursed her lips. "Maybe, I know Westmound pays a fair wage, but I don't think they pay the kind of salary to buy fourteen-thousand-dollar boots."

Tiger's jaw dropped. "Shut the front door! He paid how much for shoes? That's the stupidest thing I have ever heard. He mentioned that he's going on a two-week cruise in New Zealand with his girlfriend from the company in a few months."

I snickered, glad that he agreed M.C.'s spending

habits were ludicrous. "Lifestyles of the rich and famous, eh? He said that basically everyone had a motive to kill his dad. That Bucky was mad about losing his company. That Mac made rude remarks to Orion. Minx was mad she couldn't seduce his dad. Kandi was fooling around. Nothing earth shattering, though he was right about Kandi."

Tiger's eyebrows knitted together. "Minx tried to seduce Mac and failed? Neither of those two things sound right. I don't think Minx would go for him, and I heard he would hit any skirt that let him."

Mary twirled her pen. "She says that she thought Mac was making a legitimate sponsorship offer. They were looking into starting a recurve sight line at the company. He flew her out, gave her a tour, *et cetera*. Then he made a move on her in his office, and Kandi broke it up when she busted into the room. Then Minx left."

Thinking of unwanted advances reminded me of something. "I can totally see it happening that way. I didn't tell you, but when I showed Mac to the room by the bathrooms, he slapped me on the butt and offered me... um... I'm not sure what he was offering exactly, but I'm assuming it was sexual. So I could see him doing something similar to Minx. She's a cutie."

Tiger grinned widely and nodded. "Mmm-hmm. What's the deal with Mac destroying Bucky's company? That sounds vaguely familiar."

"Good, maybe you can explain it to me. Bucky says that Mac must have bribed someone in the rules committee for the bowhunting division."

Tiger cut me off. "Bowhunter division. They aren't actually hunting. It is just the name of a division. I think I do remember what you are talking about. There was a sudden change of rules right before the season started. Everyone had to buy new equipment, and MacSights was the only place that had sights that really took advantage of the new rules. See, in the bowhunter division there are all these rules about adjust—"

I returned the favor and cut him off. "I don't need to know the nitty-gritty of the rule changes."

He chuckled. "That's okay, I never really understood it. They have a million divisions, and I can't keep the equipment rules straight."

"I don't remember there being a million different divisions." I had only competed a little bit in high school and then all through college, but in my memory, there were only two divisions: recurve and compound.

"It's a different organization than what we're training for now. There are several different ones in the United States, but our organization doesn't have a bowhunter division. I can explain it all to you some time when you have several hours and a desire to learn all the acronyms."

"Sure. Let's schedule that for never. Tiger, Bucky said that something was shady about the rule changes. What do you think?"

"Totally. People were super upset and were signing petitions. They said they would review the decision but not until halfway through the season. People were forced to buy new sights. Conspiracy theories were running wild that MacSights was behind it. They must have made a buttload of money. Everyone bought one of their sights; probably why M.C. is walking around on the biggest waste of money on earth." Tiger shook his head in disbelief.

"I thought Bucky was being dramatic, but maybe not." I leaned over to study the list. "What is the deal with Kandi and Cold? Do guys talk about that kinda thing?"

Tiger chuckled. "Depends. I don't need to brag about all the beautiful ladies that I've spent time with.

But I've a feeling that Cold is the other type of guy."

"If you are a paragon of virtue, then we're in big trouble. What do you know about Cold?"

"He used to be a pro 3D shooter. Good but probably wasn't making a living; few do. At some point, he switched over to filming the 3D circuit instead of competing. Posting live scoring for the pro divisions, took videos, and so on. He gets sponsored by companies to cover his expenses and has built quite a following. I think he makes a solid living now. I hear he is expanding his archery coverage. I grabbed a few drinks with him at the Vegas tournament. He definitely thinks he's a big deal."

Mary muttered under her breath, "Jackwagon."

The door of the conference room banged open, and Indy and Mouse stood there.

I leaped out of my chair. "Why would you do that? Don't go around throwing doors open."

"We decorated cookies for you." Mouse extended a plate.

Feeling like a total jerk, I took a deep breath before replying. "Sorry, I didn't mean to snap."

They brought over the cookies, and Mouse placed them on the table before tucking back under Indy's arm.

The blank angel cookies we had seen earlier were now decorated in long flowing gowns. Some of the gowns were solid colors hastily smeared over the entire cookie while others were a mix of colors with sprinkles accenting certain areas.

"These are beautiful. Where did you get the supplies? Mouse, did you make these?" I pointed to the carefully crafted dresses with ornate accents.

"We found all the supplies in the refrigerator, but I made these ones." She pointed the angels of red smeared hastily across the top. "Indy did the pretty ones."

Indy ducked his head, his bangs falling across his eyes.

"They're really nice, Indy. Do you make icing dresses often?"

He laughed. "No, it was my first time, but it was fun and tasty. I'm crazy into drawing. You know that Minx is the one that got me started in art, right?"

"Oh really? Tell us." Maybe we could get some information about Cold from him plus I was genuinely interested.

He pulled a table around sideways so he could sit on it and face us. He patted the spot next to him and

Mouse joined him. Her ears poked out through her hair, and her bangs fell over half her face.

"A while ago, my dad, Cold, dated Minx. I lived with my grandparents but I got to hang out with her once. Dad told her that I liked to draw, so she brought me an art set, and we drew together. I sent her a few pictures after that, and she always wrote thank you notes with a photo of the drawing hanging on her wall. It meant a lot of me. She told me that she still has them. She's so cool. Plus, she slapped Kandi. That was awesome."

I exchanged a quick smile with Mary—this was going well. I hadn't put together that Indy's dad was Cold until now, but I should have. "Don't like Kandi, do you?"

"Gah, not at all. Dad dated her, as well. I would spend time with him in summer, and one year, she was there. She talked down to me, tried to discipline me, and took Dad away from me during my time with him. One time, I was playing my video games, but she wanted us to go to the mall. I refused, and she said I was mouthing-off. She reached up, and I thought she was going to hit me." Indy pulled a face.

"What happened?"

"Dad grabbed her hand and hauled her out of the room. She left after that, and Dad and I hung out the rest of my vacation."

"Wow. That's awful. Was this the first time that you saw her again?"

"Yep, she looks rough."

I coughed delicately. I was not a big fan of judging people on their outsides, but I hadn't heard anything about her insides to make me think it was any better. I looked around to see if anyone would pick up the ball on the conversation.

Indy saw my attention wandering off and offered up more. "But I think she wants my dad back. She's been calling him for the past month or two."

"How do you know that?"

"I've lived with my dad since fall. I didn't want to go to college, so Dad's helping me figure it out. That is why I'm here this weekend. I was going to see about the OSA program, and Dad pulled some strings to let me come this weekend, but I would rather go help him film tournaments this spring. He is working on expanding his tournament coverage, and he really needs me to help him."

Indy's face lit up when he talked about his dad.

Cold wasn't that great of a guy, but maybe he was a good father.

"I wonder why she's calling?" I let the question dangle.

"She totally wants my dad back. Says she's poor and whatever, but she's no good."

There wasn't much more I could ask without pointing out that his dad was a jackwagon. It didn't seem right to do anything that would undercut the respect he had for his dad, no matter my opinion.

"What about you, Mouse? What's your deal?"

"I was home-schooled so that I could shoot archery. I graduated early so I could train more. I applied to be an OSA, but I'm not sure." It all came out in a rush directed at the floor behind her dangling feet. She flicked her eyes to look at Indy then cast them down at the floor.

"Okay, well, thanks for the cookies. They are delicious."

"Yeah, yeah, yeah," Indy said. He hopped off the table and reached for Mouse's hand. "I bet the game is finished downloading. We're gonna go."

After they left the room, I picked up a cookie. "I can barely stand to eat it. They are really nice."

Mary leaned over and snagged it from my hand. "I'll take care of that for you." She bit into it. "Mmm, beautiful and tasty."

Minx poked her head in the door. "Here you are. Someone shoot me now."

Mary pulled out a chair and patted the seat. "How did it go?"

"Awful, just awful. The absolute worst. It was like being five and screwing up all over again, but I'm an adult and should know better. Elizabeth wasn't mad; she was just disappointed in my behavior." Minx walked past the chair and instead lay down on the floor facedown in despair. "I'm the biggest failure ever."

Mary raced over and patted her head. "No, you're not a failure. You just... um..."

She looked at me for help. I didn't have much comfort to offer. Minx had been difficult since she'd arrived and gotten into a lady tussle. I tried to add some encouragement. "Indy thinks it's cool that you slapped Kandi."

Minx pushed up on her elbows to look at me. "Great, does he have a training center that I can work and live at?"

Mary sat down crossed-legged. "Oh no, did they

turn you down?"

"Not yet. They said they will have to take everything into consideration, but I know what that means."

"I'll put in a good word for you. And so will Di."

Mary had always had a fondness for Minx that outweighed my own. Her humor often crossed over into rude, she could be difficult to communicate with, and she'd given me a nickname I hated. I also knew from experience that I didn't want to damage my reputation by hitching my cart to an unstable horse. "I'm sure they won't ask my opinion."

"Guys, I know I was all, 'I can be Daphne from Scooby-doo and help solve the crime,' but I really don't want to right now. Would anyone mind if I went to my room and showered? I have cried too many times today, and I feel gross."

We still had a killer roaming around somewhere. "This might be a weird suggestion, but I think you should take Tiger with you be—"

Tiger cut me off. "Awesome, I approve."

I gave him a stern look, but I couldn't keep the smile off my lips. "Because I really don't think anyone should be alone."

138

"Plus, I could scrub your back." Tiger gave Minx wink.

Minx rolled off her stomach into a sitting position then stood up. "Tiger can come, but no back scrubbing. We clear?" Minx rolled off her stomach into a sitting position then stood up. "Tiger can come, but no back scrubbing. We clear?"

Tiger gave a gigantic sigh, but from the look in his eye, I bet he would try to convince Minx a few more times to share a shower. "I suppose so."

Death at the Summit

CHAPTER ELEVEN

After a few minutes, Mary and I walked into the hallway. I was busy talking to Mary and didn't notice that I was about to run into Cold until she grabbed my elbow.

I gasped. "Sorry, Cold, I wasn't expecting anyone."

Cold sneered at me while Kandi hovered behind him. "Whatever, Kandi wants to ask you something." He turned to her. "Geez, we found them. Go ahead and ask."

She had a wide smile on her face. "The bathrooms we used earlier had a shower in them. I was hoping to use one."

"I'm going back to the dining room." Cold threw over his shoulder as he left.

She turned to watch him leave, the smile slipping as her eyes narrowed. She turned back to me, the big, fake smile back in place.

No way was I going to offer her our shower. I didn't want her in our room, free to poke through our things, or even worse, be naked in my bathroom. I would need to bleach the entire place before I could shower again. And obviously, the bathrooms she'd used earlier were still off limits until Mac's body was removed. "Those bathrooms are closed off. Sorry."

"There are other bathrooms, on the gun side of the center," Mary offered. She was a nicer person than I was to find a solution.

I turned to Kandi. "Oh, I forgot about those. Do you need anything to shower?"

Kandi patted a huge designer bag covered in logos hanging off an arm. "Like all women, I keep everything I need in here."

"You carry soap with you?" I didn't think I had anything like that in my purse.

She looked at me, puzzled. "Soap, a hand towel, make up and several pairs of extra undies. You don't?"

"Several pairs?" slipped out before I could stop myself. There are several reasons that someone might need to carry several pairs, and all were private reasons.

Kandi rolled her eyes at me. "I should have known

by looking at you two that you wouldn't understand. If you ever want to learn how to get ahead in life, let me know. I'll show you how to use your real *assets*. Especially you, Mary, you're young and have that exotic oriental thing going on."

"I'm from Minnesota. Plus, rugs are oriental. People are Asian," Mary said.

Kandi rolled her eyes again. "Whatever."

As we walked down the hallways, the answer to the question of whether Kandi was looking rough or not was obvious. The promotion images on the MacSight booth had been heavily altered. Thin lines from the corner of her eyes, like the kind starting around my own, showed her as slightly older and the dull orangey tint of her skin indicated a spray-tanning obsession. Her hair had a thick section dyed a brassy, unnatural red, which offset the dull-blond section. Overall, her hair had been processed to the breaking point. Her breasts were high and close together, with deep vertical wrinkles between them; her ribs were visible. I tried to look past the heavy makeup slathered on her, but it was hard to see through that many layers.

Her husband had been killed earlier that day. She deserved some kindness. "How are you holding up?"

"Fine, I guess. It's been really tough, but I'll get the money soon then buy it back."

We walked on for a few strides. Her answer soaked in, and it didn't fit the question I'd asked. I stopped and blinked. "What?"

She stopped and blinked back as though we were in competition to see who was more confused. She gasped with dawning realization. "Oh that, I'm doing okay. I can't believe I'm a widow." Her tone was hard to place—was she sad or excited to be a widow?

But more than anything, I was curious about what she wanted to buy back. "What did you think I meant?"

Kandi twisted her hair into a bun and grabbed a hair stick out of her bag. Inserting the stick and tugging on the bun to check that it was secure, she continued, "I thought you were asking about me losing Kandi-covered. It's not fair that it got sold to Westmound; it's mine. I'm Kandi. I *am* Kandi-covered."

"Wow, that's awful. I have to admit that I only started working in the archery industry a few months ago, and I'm not familiar with Kandi-covered."

She was on a roll and eager to talk. "Kandi-covered is a product line of women's clothing, bumper stickers, hats, *et cetera*. Plus, we worked with companies to create branded Kandi-covered products. So, for instance, my first product was a Kandi-covered MacSight. We took an existing product and branded it with pink camo pattern, marked up the price a little, and sold it. We started with the pink camo but expanded into teal, lime green, salmon pink, *et cetera* and added cheetah, tiger, and a few other patterns. Once the Kandi-covered MacSights sold, I added other partnerships to product line: mechanical releases, bows, quivers, and so forth. I wanted to have my own company, so I told Mac I wanted to start Kandi-covered. Have it be my own project; do all the marketing materials, generate contacts, everything. He got me all set up and told me it was all mine. I had no idea that it legally belonged to MacSights. When he sold the company, Kandi-covered was sold, too. I have never been so mad in my entire life." She looked at me, waiting for a reply.

"Oh, no."

"Yes, then it was too late. I designed clothing: hats, yoga pants, jackets, everything. I knew everything involved with Kandi-covered from social media to finances. I once caught a two-cent error in the books. I turned a profit every quarter and reinvested all the profits back into the brand. When Mac sold MacSights,

Kandi-covered was the most profitable part of the company, and the deal was dependent on it being included. I had no idea Kandi-covered was tied into MacSights. He said he would take care of me, and he screwed that up."

"That's really impressive, Kandi. I'm so sorry about your company."

"Let that be a lesson to you both. Never trust a man to take care of you. Never. No one will take care of you but you. Get what you can from them, and you can get a lot if you play it right, but in the end, the only one you can trust is you."

We arrived at the bathroom door. After unlocking the door, I reached inside to flip the switch and give the bathroom a once-over. "Here you go. Anything else you need?"

"No, thank you. If you girls ever want to raise your image, you would be great for the Kandi-covered brand. Once I buy it back, that is."

This might be my last chance to sneak in some questions. "How are you going to get it back? Will you get anything from Mac?"

"Nothing. He was mortgaged to the hilt and in debt up to his eyeballs. I had no idea when we got married that he was in such bad financial shape. Next time, I'm getting a credit check before I say, 'I do.' He's been on the edge of bankruptcy for years. Don't you worry about me; I'll land on my feet and get it all back before you know it." She pulled the door shut behind her, and the clap of a deadbolt filled the hallways.

"Wow," Mary said as we walked away. "That was kinda…"

"Bitter? Weird? Heartless?"

"Sad. That's not normal, is it?"

I put an arm around her, pulling her in close. Moo wedged himself between us. "Nothing about Kandi is normal. I'm going through a divorce, and I still believe in love. Plus, you have awesome parents that have a great marriage. You'll never be like Kandi."

We followed the hallway around a corner and ran into Jess. She was smiling and looked more relaxed than she had last time I had seen her. Her freak-out meter had gone down from code red to a respectable yellow.

"Glad I found you two. Elizabeth wants to talk to you."

I gave Mary's shoulder a few quick squeezes then dropped my arm. "Is she ticked about the murder?"

"I'll let her ask you, but it's not about the murder. I

can't wait until the police get here, and I can go lay down. Robbie went back to the hotel with the buses to prepare for tomorrow and finish up his meetings. Now he is stuck over there." Robbie was her husband and director of the center. The firearms staff and Robbie had taken responsibility for the hotel portion of the summit while Jess and the archery staff took over range day.

Unfortunately, range day had turned into one long responsibility.

We walked down the hallway toward Jess's office. The door next to hers, the conference room that the firearms side of the center used for their meetings, was open. It was a large room with whiteboards and rows of tables and chairs, much like the archery conference room. The windows lining the far wall showed a dim landscape with thick snowflakes floating to the ground in a curtain of white. Loggin, Orion, Liam, and Elizabeth were inside, around a table. Loggin looking pleased, and everyone called out a greeting to us.

Elizabeth stood and joined us in the hallway and we went down to Jessica's office. Elizabeth first asked to speak to Mary, alone then after a minute, she excused Mary and asked me in.

Stepping inside, I shut the door behind Moo and me. Moo settled in next to me, then I faced Elizabeth.

"I want to know your opinion on having Minx as an On-Site Athlete. You will be working with her and have worked with her."

So much for no one caring about my opinion. I opened my mouth then shut it. I took a breath to speak then stopped again. I wasn't sure what to say. I could give a pat answer that she would be great, but I didn't want to stand behind that answer when I had concerns.

Elizabeth addressed my obvious hesitation. "I know that you ran a tech company for years. I want your honest, management opinion."

"Technically, I didn't run it all alone, but I know what you mean. Let me think about it for a second." I sat back in the chair and sorted through my thoughts and feelings. I had strong opinions on hiring. When I first hired people, I relied heavily on things like GPA and grades, but eventually discovered that there were others things that mattered more like work ethic, flexibility, communication, and being easy to work with. "Are you sure that you want me to speak freely?"

"Absolutely, that's why you're here."

I took a deep breath and sent up a prayer that

honesty was the right way to go. "I think it depends on what you are looking for with the OSAs. Minx is an incredibly talented archer, but she's also a bit of a mess. She got in one physical fight tonight and then yelled at Loggin. I've worked with her twice, and for what it's worth, we clashed. If you are looking for someone already at the peak of their career with their life together, that's not her, but......" I trailed off. Everything I had said was fact; the next bit was supposition.

"But?"

"But if you are interested in developing employees, then I think Minx is a solid bet. She's in a rough place in life, but with good mentoring, I think she could develop into an amazing return on investment. She recently learned that meeting her goal of attending the Summer Games hasn't magically transformed her life. I know that I've been there—success doesn't automatically equal happiness. In fact, it can do the opposite, you know?"

Elizabeth nodded. "I do. Go on."

"Mary has a lot of faith in Minx, and I have faith in Mary. I think..." I hesitated, wanting to make sure that I really believed in what I was saying. "I think that despite my personal conflicts with Minx and some of her behavior today, that if this is something she really wants then she could benefit from the program."

Elizabeth smiled. "Thank you, Di, I'm very impressed."

"Why?"

"I know that you and Minx have issues, but it's great to see that you can be objective and think big picture. You have a natural flare for it. I would love to see you get involved in some of our leadership training someday." She stood up.

I followed suit, beaming with pleasure at the compliment. When I left the company I had owned with my soon-to-be ex-husband, I had given up on the idea of ever being in a leadership role again. I had felt empty and deflated. But now I was building myself up again, and doors were starting to open. I reached out and shook her hand enthusiastically. "Thank you, Elizabeth. Is there anything else you need?"

"No, that was it. Jess and I need to get back to the group to finish off that meeting."

We stepped into the hallway.

"Did they ask you about Minx?" Mary moved in close to my side as Elizabeth and Jess walked by to the conference room.

"Yes, but I think it was more of a test of me than it was about Minx." I was buoyed by Elizabeth's praise as we headed back into the main archery hallways of the center. I spotted Minx and Tiger coming in the entrance, and we jogged down the hallways to meet up with them.

"Back already?"

Minx ran her hand through her wet, red hair. "I didn't want to give Tiger any ideas by hanging out too long with him alone."

We snickered and started walking down the hallway. I stuck my head in my office as we passed. "How are things going in here?"

Indy and Mouse were squished in tight. Indy looked up. "Awesome, Mouse is totally leet. We're killing noobs left and right. Hey, Minx, you wanna see?"

Minx pushed past me. "I would love to. Tell me about it."

She pulled a chair up behind them, and Indy started pointing and rattling off facts to Minx. Mouse's eyes narrowed a little as she scooted in closer to Indy.

Moo whined next to me and scratched my leg with one gigantic paw. I knelt next to him to scratch his face.

"What's up, buddy?"

He let out a long warbling groan and pawed me again.

Mary pulled out her phone. "Hey, look at the time."

Seeing that we had significantly missed Moo's dinner time, I was thankful he wasn't chewing my leg off. "I need to go"——I covered Moo's ears and whispered the next two words— "feed Moo. How bad is it out there?"

Tiger turned to look down the hallway toward the entrance. "Not too bad. The snow is letting up some. I'll walk you guys over there."

CHAPTER TWELVE

I got Moo all fed, and this time, I remembered to warn everyone about Moo's rough play in the snow. The sky was darkening as we walked back toward the center. The snow still fell heavily, but the visibility was much better. Hopefully, that meant the snow plows would be here soon, closely followed by the police. I had debated hiding in my room, far away from Mac's body and his murderer, but Mary was being so brave that I didn't want to admit I was uncomfortable.

"Thanks for escorting us, Tiger. That was very gentlemanly of you," Mary said as she clasped the elbow he had offered.

I hung on his other side for balance and a bit of warmth. We opened the center door, and Moo pushed in ahead of us, shaking the loose snow off his vest.

I let go of Tiger's arm and headed down the

hallway. "If we hurry, we might be able to catch Cold alone." I ducked my head into my office. "Minx, you still doing okay? We're going to take care of some stuff."

Minx looked up. "I'm gonna stay here with Indy and Mouse. Hang out with my little bro some more."

Indy looked back over his shoulder at Minx with a big smile. "That would be great, big sis."

Mouse relaxed a little, and a small smile crept onto her face when Indy said "big sis." She turned around to Minx. "Do you want to play for a while?"

Stepping into the hallway, I turned to Tiger one last time. "Are you sure you are up to this?"

"Yes, I can handle asking Cold a few questions."

We rounded the corner and approached the dining room entrance. I peeked around the edge, and Cold was sitting alone with his back to the entrance. He certainly wasn't worried about anyone sneaking up on him, and that worked to our advantage. The dining room had a half wall around the edge of the tables.

I ducked back. "If Mary and I can get over to the half wall without Cold seeing us, then we could listen. Tiger, you watch. Mary, come with me."

I crouched low and raced over on the balls on my

feet. Mary was silent behind me, but I had forgotten about Moo, who thought we were playing a game. He bounded back and forth then got down low and knocked me over. Doing my best action-hero roll, I managed to get to the spot I'd picked with only minimal rug burns on each arm and a sore knee. I grimaced and rubbed the spots, waiting for the sting to subside. Mary came in next to me.

At the entrance, Tiger shook his head. Then he entered and called out, "Hey, Cold, good to see you."

From over the wall, we heard Cold reply, "Hey, man, good to see you. Come sit with me. How much longer until we can get out of here?"

The reply was lost when Mary leaned in close and whispered, "Are you okay?"

"Fine. I thought I handled that roll pretty well."

She grimaced. "Uh, it was not your most graceful moment, loose arms and legs everywhere. You sure you didn't dislocate something?"

So much for being an action hero. I rubbed my hands over my body, and everything felt like it was in the right spot. "I'll probably be sore tomorrow, but I'm fine. Thanks for the concern, but…" I pointed up at the conversation between Cold and Tiger going on over our head.

Cold was bragging…"On top of all of that, I'll be coming to a few of your events. 3D archery has really taken off since I started covering it, and whoever runs your type of tournaments practically begged me to promote them, as well. We'll see if we can get the terms worked out. As the voice of the archery industry, I want to do what I can to help, but I can't be giving handouts."

Mary stuck a finger in her mouth and fake-gagged. I held back a laugh as Tiger continued.

"Cool, cool, sounds like you're doing great. Can you believe there was a murder today?"

"I could've told you that someone was going to kill that old geezer off eventually. He pissed everyone off. I didn't work with him 'cause he was cheaper than a two-dollar hooker. You know who I think did it? Loggin. When I'm filming, sometimes the guys forget I'm there, and I get all sorts of stuff recorded. I like to keep it in my back pocket for a rainy day. Loggin has been whining all season about some money he's owed."

"I don't know Loggin. What's he like?"

A sound of a body shifting around in a seat was audible before Cold answered, "He's some hot-shot college athlete that had an injury, knee or ankle or something. He follows the rules and is a regular Boy Scout." His tone sounded disappointed. I could imagine a snarl on his face.

"Do Boy Scouts commit lots of murders?" Tiger joked.

"Anyone could commit a murder. It's not so hard."

The hairs on my arm raised, and I scooted in close to Mary. I was regretting this conversation. Was Tiger in danger?

"Oh, yeah, of course." Tiger didn't sound convinced. "What about Kandi?"

"She could have killed him or not. Anyone could have killed him— you, that uptight computer chick, M.C., anyone."

"You?"

"What motive do I have? I'm just here filming. No idea how I got caught up in this whole thing."

"I heard that you and Kandi have a thing going on. Maybe you wanted her to yourself?"

"Oh, is that getting around? I'm not surprised she's bragging about it. Let me tell you though, if you're getting the milk for free while some other dude is paying for the cow's upkeep, do you off the owner? Of course not." His laughter was loud and long.

I leaned closer to Mary and whispered, "Cold and Kandi deserve each other."

She nodded back and petted Moo. His formidable tail started wagging against the floor with heavy whomps. I grabbed it as soon as possible and held my breath.

"Did you hear something?" Cold asked.

"Probably just the pipes." Tiger's voice was a tight and high. He quickly changed the topic. "Why do you think someone killed Mac?"

"Why do you care? It was probably sex or money. Hey, it's been great catching up, but I am ready to go. I'm gonna find that cop and see about getting out of here."

Mary clenched my arm. "What do we do now?"

I hadn't really thought about how we could get out. We couldn't see him, and there was no way to tell when the coast was clear. If he started to exit and saw us here, then he would know we'd been listening.

Brian rounded the corner, saw us sitting up against the wall, and rolled his eyes. He gestured us to one side. "Cold, if you are ready, I can interview you."

As Cold came into sight, Brian moved to his far

side, constantly talking to Cold, keeping his attention pointed away from us before stepping into the hallway and out of sight.

I let out the breath I was holding and stood up, dusting myself off. "That was close."

Brian's voice in the hallway was raised in a shout. "Just go down to the corner and wait for me there." He stuck his head back into the cafeteria. "That's the opposite of staying out of trouble. When I am done talking to Cold, I want to talk to both of you. Got that?"

We nodded and he disappeared back down one of the hallways.

"Geez, of course he would catch us."

Tiger ran a hand through his hair. "When he started to leave, I freaked out a little bit. I don't trust him, and I'm not sure what he would do if he caught you."

"Hi, guys."

I whipped around to see Kandi had joined us. "Hi, Kandi," I said, but she was looking past me at Tiger.

"I was hoping to grab some food from the kitchen, but with a murderer running around, I am too scared to be alone. Tiger, could you come with me?" She crossed her arms and rubbed her hands down them, pushing her cleavage to dangerous heights.

Tiger's eyes were lowered and locked on target. "Of course, Kandi, I wasn't doing anything anyways."

"So much for having Tiger help us." I said to Mary after they went into the cafeteria.

"That's fine. We only have one person left on the list: Loggin."

"Did I hear my name?"

I turned around and Loggin had snuck up on us. "Yes, I was wondering how you got your name. We were about to sit down. Did you want to join us?" I gestured to the empty room.

Loggin took two huge strides, placed a hand on the half wall, and bounded over it. "Love to."

Mary and I took the long way around to join him.

"My name's an accident. When I started competing, I would make tons of posts about my training schedule like 'Logging in at the range' or 'Logging in at the weight room.' No one warned me that people were obsessed with nicknames, and next thing I knew…" He shrugged and pulled up another chair to prop up his legs.

I couldn't help but notice an attitude change from earlier today. "You sure are chipper. Did you get everything worked out?"

"Pretty much. Few more details to iron out, but I'm confident it will get taken care of."

"I think after the way you snapped at us this morning, we deserve an explanation." I tried to keep my voice light and teasing with a big smile on my face as I said it.

"Sure, why not? Little over a year ago, I met Mac from MacSights, and we started talking about being a sponsored shooter with a contingency plan."

I interrupted. "What's contingency?"

"They agree to pay you if you get a certain placement or better at tournaments on their list. It's a pretty standard setup between pro archers and their sponsors. It's a rare archer that gets paid just to be on staff. MacSights is a big company that does really well, so I figured they would be solid. We hammered out a great plan. It wasn't that great if I did okay, but if I placed in the top three, it paid very well. So I trained hard. First tournament of the season, in Vegas, I won. That's a huge pay-out. I get these gigantic novelty checks from my sponsors, including MacSights, but when I get home, the check from MacSights bounces. It's like six months' rent."

"Ouch, did you find out what happened?"

"I call Mac first thing. I thought he was being honest when he said that he had no clue how that happened. He said he would take care of it. I figure that he's legit. I decide that I'll do the entire 3D schedule and every other tournament I can, which is a big commitment, but with the Vegas money, I should be able to swing it. I quit my job so I could train and travel. I had my entire budget worked out, but it was based on getting that Vegas money from MacSights."

"Oh oh, I think I see where this is going." I chewed on a fingernail.

"Yes, it seems obvious in hindsight but I have a good excuse. The next tournament I placed and got a much smaller check from MacSights, and that one went through, so I figured they would be good on their word. They sent the big check again a couple months later, and it bounced again. Mac made excuses again, but all the smaller checks I was getting were legit. But without the money, I had to give up my apartment. I just couldn't get the ends to meet, and I was halfway across the country competing. Do you know how embarrassing it is to move back in with your parents? All my stuff is sitting in their garage right now while I work this out."

"Hey, me, too. My circumstances are a bit different, but most of my stuff is sitting in their garage in Texas right now while I work here and finalize my divorce."

He reached across the table and offered up his hand for a fist bump. "You know this sucks. I got three bounced checks, and my bank was starting to look at me sideways. Then Mac starts dodging my phone calls. I'm still trying to practice full time, compete, and get my life back home squared away. I couldn't even afford to fly home to move out of my apartment; my brothers had to do it for me. Do you know how much I owe them? I'll be stuck helping them move until the day I die."

"That sucks. Did you ever get an explanation from Mac?"

"I don't know what happened, except that one day, like a month ago, I call, and Mac says that they were bought out by Westmound and it was no longer his responsibility. He tries to claim that it was an unrecoverable debt and I should write it off on my taxes."

"Whoa, is that how it works?" Something didn't seem right about that.

"No idea, probably not, but he blocked my number. The secretary wouldn't put me through, and I couldn't afford an attorney. I tried getting ahold of Westmound, but they couldn't do a lot to help me yet since MacSights was in the process of being purchased. I didn't want to talk about it too much because I didn't want to get a reputation of bad-mouthing sponsors. But when I heard about this event, I figured I could drive over and crash it. If I could just talk to someone high up, I could get them to listen."

"And?"

"And it totally worked. No thanks to Mac."

"You're still pretty mad at him. Did you see him today?"

Loggin chuckled. He wadded up a napkin from the dispenser and bounced it between his hands. "I know what you're getting at, and no, I didn't kill him. That wouldn't get me the money he owes me, and that was my goal. I'll tell you who I think did it—M.C. or Kandi. He was a crook so they were probably crooks, too." He swatted the napkin hard, and it sailed over two tables and landed neatly in a lone coffee cup.

He leaped out of his chair, arms held high. "Did you see that? That was awesome." He did a quick little dance that reminded me of a football player after a touchdown.

I couldn't help but laugh. Mary giggled, as well. He was a fun guy when he wasn't sulking around.

He finished his dance and turned back to us. "So, I still need to apologize to the little red-head, you heard my story so now you owe me." He turned a smile on us that probably got him whatever he wanted.

"Okay, come on. She's down the hallway. Come on, Moo."

We got up to leave, and Loggin played with Moo, asking questions about him. Moo seemed very fond of Loggin, and that was probably a better indicator of his character than anything Loggin could have said.

As we passed the conference room, Liam called out my name. With a huge smile, I told Mary and Loggin on go on without me while I ducked into the conference room.

"Hey, I've barely seen you all day. How are you holding up?" I asked Liam as I pulled a chair out across from him. A noise from out in the hall brought my head up, but it didn't happen again, and I focused on Liam.

"Pretty well."

He seemed a bit more distant than normal, which was saying something because he was quiet in the best of times. I cast around for something to discuss. "So

167

you and Orion are good friends? Did you meet when he started working at Westmound?"

"No, we were college roommates."

"Oh, random chance?"

"A little bit. We were on the same floor my freshman year. He's a year older. There was a big group of us that liked to go jog, hike, or play sports together, and second semester, we took an elective together. Beginning Film, I think it was called, and we did a group project together. Basically everyone bailed but us."

"What kind of project was it?"

"Short film. There were two girl parts. At one point, I complained about having to wear a dress, and Orion said, 'If it's good enough for Eddie Murphy and Robin Williams, then you can suck it up.'" Liam chuckled at the memory. Whatever had been weighing him down was disappearing.

"How did it go?"

"It was pretty awful but good enough to pass. But more than anything, we realized that we had each other's back."

"And he got a job at Westmound after he graduated?"

Liam nodded. "In spring of my junior year, my dad

died suddenly. Grandpa had passed away like six months earlier, and Mom was already overloaded with that. She wasn't sleeping or eating. I thought she was going to die of a broken heart. I never went back to school."

I nodded along, and he continued.

"Orion packed up our apartment with all my stuff I left behind and drove it to my mom's house in Salt Lake and basically moved in."

"How did he end up working at Westmound?"

"Mom told him that if he wanted to start at the bottom and work his way up, that was an option. She obviously had a ton of respect for him. Few people want to start at the bottom, but Orion was thrilled to. That's what I did, as well. We have done almost every job at Westmound. Assembling equipment, sales, marketing, *et cetera*. Trust me, Orion has his current job because he earned it."

He was quiet for a second, staring off into space before he stood. "I need to go."

As he got up to leave, I realized he might be able to solve a mystery. "Liam, when Westmound bought MacSights, did you do a financial audit?"

"Of course we did, and it's interesting. If you want

to take I look, I'll send it over. Hey, M.C., you need something?" Liam was looking beyond me.

I twisted around to look at the conference room entrance to see M.C. leaning in the door.

"Just wondering where the bathrooms are?" he asked with a strained smile.

I pointed in the general direction of the entrance where the bathrooms were located next to the front desk. He gave a wave as he walked away.

I looked back at Liam. "I guess the huge bathroom sign in the hallway needs to be about three times bigger."

As we exited the room, we ran into Brian.

"Where's M.C. off to?" Brian ran a hand through his hair, looking exhausted.

"To the bathroom," I answered

"Not unless he is planning to go in the parking lot. He just raced out the entrance."

CHAPTER THIRTEEN

I ran down the hallway toward the entrance, with Brian close behind. I passed Minx and Loggin chatting on the floor of the hallway, and Mary let out a startled, "What's going on?" as I ran past my office. I hit the entrance doors hard and burst into the clear night.

The snow had stopped, and the sky was clear overhead, a solid blanket of black and twinkling stars. The air bit into my skin immediately. They said that the clearer the sky, the colder it was in winter. There were footsteps in the snow interrupted by a huge mess in the otherwise-smooth snow—it looks like a snow angel created by someone with no control over their limbs. The footsteps continued again then halted into another failed snow angel.

Mary pushed out the door next to me and followed my gaze. "I guess those fourteen-thousand dollar boots aren't good for running in the snow."

Minx, who came out the door with Loggin, pointed out across the empty field. "There he is. Why is he running like that?"

M.C. was barely visible in the parking lot lights. He was running with a wide-legged pace, as though he were smuggling bricks in his pants.

"I think he is trying to keep from falling over again. But where is he going? It's freezing, and there is nothing that direction for hundreds of miles."

Suddenly, Moo took off. Huge galloping strides tore across the distance between him and M.C.

Tiger and Kandi stepped up to join the group. I took a deep breath and started to call after Moo, but Liam shushed me.

"Let Moo take care of this."

Our group huddled close to watch Moo as he caught up to M.C. and hit him from behind. M.C. went down hard. Moo danced around him, jumping on his back, looking to play.

I rubbed my hands together in the cold air. "Jinkies! I think we found the killer."

Brian burst out laughing, and after he caught his breath, he turned to us and said in an over-the-top stern voice, "And he might have gotten away with it if it wasn't for you meddling kids and dog named Scooby-Moo."

We laughed and groaned in unison.

Brian jogged away, snickering to himself. "I've been waiting for that all day."

Kandi looked around the group. "What just happened?"

"We know who killed your husband."

"But why?" She asked, snuggling under Cold's arm after he came out to join us.

"That's a good question."

***

It had been a week since M.C. had been arrested, and I still wanted answers. After Brian handcuffed him, the snowplows and police had arrived. The rest of the Westmound Summit was relaxing after that.

I finished packing a light suitcase for my trip home. I was going to Texas to be with my parents for a short Christmas break. Jess was taking me to the airport in a few hours, but first, I needed to take care of two gifts.

Walking to the center, I passed Brian in his squad car. I gave him a wave around the packages I juggled in my arms.

He rolled down his window. "Di, come here for a second."

I maneuvered closer to his vehicle. "You gonna tell me all about the murder?"

He chuckled. "You'll want to talk to Liam. I had a question about why you asked me if Mac was poisoned. Did you see or hear something?"

The memory card was long gone. I swallowed hard. "No, nothing. Why?"

He examined my face closely. "The coroner had some suspicions. I'm not sure if they will follow up on anything, but if you had some evidence to share…"

I shook my head. "No evidence."

"Okay then. See you after Christmas." He rolled up his window and drove off.

Brian had been scarce since the arrest, but the fact that he had been here today hopefully meant that he had some news to share. I stepped into the center and jogged down the hallway of the center until I reached the equipment room.

Knocking on the door, I saw Liam working at the far side of the room. I called out, "Did you get any dirt from Brian?"

Liam turned around and waved me in. Moo came

over for scratches. I don't know what I was going to do not seeing their fuzzy faces daily.

"I did. And it explains a lot of things. Now, don't repeat this to anyone."

I crossed my heart. "I promise, no one except maybe Mary."

He chuckled. "M.C. had been embezzling for years under his dad's name, but when the company sold and we did an audit, he was worried that we would catch it. If his dad was dead, then he could blame it on him. I think he freaked when he heard us talking about financial records, figured we knew something."

I laughed. "We might have figured it out eventually. Did Brian tell you how Mac was killed?"

"Only in a really vague sense. M.C. used a hunting knife on display to stab his dad and used some shirts somehow to block most of the blood. Then he rinsed off in the bathroom. If the forensics had been able to get there sooner, it would have been an easier case."

I nodded. "That's it?"

"Yep, maybe we will get more details in the future, but for now, that's all I know. Hey, I got you something."

I perked up. I had been unsure about giving him a

gift, but now I felt confident that I made the right decision. "Me too."

I extended my gifts as he turned around with a stack of company catalogues and a sandwich bag on top.

A blush crept up my neck, hot and awkward. "Oh, I thought you meant…" I had asked for information on all the companies that Westmound owned to research during my vacation. I picked up the sandwich bag with a memory card in it. I felt uneasy. "What's this?"

"The night of the murder, Moo got sick, and guess what I found?"

"A pile of vomit?"

"Yes, and it was disgusting, but there was also a memory card. I figured you would know what that meant?"

I looked at the baggy distastefully. A vomit-y memory card was new to me.

Liam chuckled and took the presents I had offered him. "And I also have this for you." He pulled out a wrapped gift about the size of a phone book and handed it to me.

I pointed to the larger box. "That one's for Moo." Anxiety knotted my stomach as I waited for his reactions to the presents.

He opened up a rubber bone and a black backpack with the words "Crime Stopper." Moo walked over to sniff the backpack then took the bone out of Mac's hand. He lay down and starting chewing on the corner.

I rushed to explain. "I read that Great Danes are working dogs, and having a job helps."

"Did you get him a job at the police station?"

"No, you put like rice or sand in the backpack, and it helps the dog to feel accomplished. Plus, he has helped solve two murders. He has earned it. Now open yours."

I held my breath as he opened up the tiny box.

First, he pulled out a wooden stand then carefully removed a marble that filled his palm. "That's awesome. There's a gun in there."

I rushed to explain. "I have a friend that works glass for a living. I sent a picture of the 1911 pistol that Westmound is introducing next season, and she made a marble. I hope you like it."

"I really do. That's amazing and very appropriate. Open yours." He carefully placed the marble on the stand, turning it until the gun was right side up.

I pulled the paper off a plastic box. On the side were sliding locks, which I undid then flipped up the top. Nestled in the foam egg crate was the same 1911 pistol that I had showed the glass artist. I gasped.

"Do you like it?" Liam stepped next to me. The tips of his ears were red.

"It's a gun. That's way too much."

"As opposed to a custom-made marble? Plus, I know someone. This is more of a target gun, but when you get back, we'll get you into the concealed carry class and hook you up with something smaller to carry daily."

I turned to him in shock. "You want me to wear a gun at work?"

He chuckled. "Di, you work at a gun range in Wyoming. You are probably the only one here not wearing a gun already. I want you to be safe. You've found two dead bodies. If you had been a bit earlier either time…" He shook his head.

A warmth fluttered in my stomach, and my cheeks were hot as I checked the time. I couldn't knock the goofy smile off my face. "I really have to get back to packing. I'll……" I swallowed. "I'll miss you both."

He opened his arms, and I stepped into his hug. Muffled into my hair, he said, "Travel safe and hurry back."

ABOUT THE AUTHOR

Nikki Haverstock lives with her husband and dogs on a cattle ranch high in the Rocky Mountains.

Before escaping the city, Nikki taught collegiate archery for ten years. She has competed on and off for fifteen in the USA Archery women's recurve division.

Nikki has more college degrees than she has sense, and hopefully one day she will put one to work.

Learn more at http://NikkiHaverstock.com

Made in the USA
Columbia, SC
23 July 2020

14511465R00117